My warmest thanks to
De Ila and Les Meyer
of Saluda Farms
for their time and help with this book.
It is dedicated to them and to the gang:
Jock
Kissyfer
Belle
and Saluda Sam.

Llamas on the Loose

by Jeri Massi

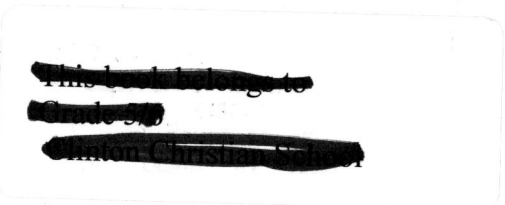

ADVENTURE SERIES

Bob Jones University Press, Greenville, South Carolina 29614

Llamas on the Loose

Edited by Olivia Tschappler

Cover and illustrations by Dana Thompson

©1988 Bob Jones University Press
Greenville, South Carolina 29614

All rights reserved

ISBN 0-89084-452-6

Printed in the United States of America

20 19 18 17 16 15 14 13 12 11 10 9

The Peabody Series

Derwood, Inc.
A Dangerous Game
Treasure in the Yukon
Courage by Darkness
Llamas on the Loose

Contents

Publisher's Note ix
1 Ticktock 1
2 Everything All at Once 9
3 Welcome to Winneca Farms 13
4 First Troubles 19
5 Settling In 25
6 An Emergency 29
7 Startling News 39
8 New Projects 49
9 A Breathless Ride 55
10 Tragedy at Night 61
11 Jean Comes Home 67
12 Night Watch 75
13 Back to Normal 81
14 The New Team 87
15 Tracking Down Clues 95
16 The Sheriff Again 105
17 Beans Has a Lesson 109
18 An Adventure Despite Precautions 115
19 We Stumble into Danger 121
20 Answers 129
21 Really a Team 135

Publisher's Note

The Peabody Series presents the adventures of a group of Christian young people from the First Bible Church of Peabody, Wisconsin. Each book focuses on a new adventure that involves several members of the youth group.

Penny, the narrator of this book, is a spokesman for the team that includes Jack and Scruggs and finally Jean. While they are trying to solve the mystery at the llama farm, Scruggs takes the lead in witnessing to Doc Ericson. But Doc makes it a point never to talk religion, and they all learn some sobering truths about people who don't want to listen.

Christian children, parents and educators have already acknowledged the Peabody Series as something refreshingly new: an incorporation of high adventure with the realistic struggles of Christian youth today. While the books show the importance of the Christian family, they also examine the conflicts that the Christian adolescent may have when he faces a difficult or unexpected situation.

Chapter One
Ticktock

Well, school would be starting in about three weeks, and I was pretty blue.

Three weeks left of summer, and nothing to do or see and no place to go. Jack and Scruggs were up in Canada in the Yukon, and even Jean was gone. I'd played the heroic big sister and had let her stay in Alabama instead of me.

The only person around who was near my age was Annette from up the street, and if you've read any of the other books about Peabody, Wisconsin, you already know why I'd still be blue. We had tried to be friends, but we drove each other crazy. I like horses and mountains and dog stories and taking long walks and exploring. Annette likes clothes and shoes, and she talks about boys and is kind of bossy and thinks dogs are dirty, and she doesn't like getting wet. And besides, she hates Scruggs and talks about him a lot and how he'll ruin Jack and turn him into a thug.

I think she's just saying what she's heard grownups say, because I know that some grownups do say things like that. But others—like my dad and like the pastor and like Mrs. Bennett—they all say that Scruggs has really changed. And I suppose they should know, especially Mrs. Bennett, because she's his foster mother now.

Anyway, I did try to defend Scruggs to Annette, and I told her that he had explained to me himself that he was a Christian just like I was. He had told me all about how he'd gotten saved and how—while he was out in San Francisco—the Lord had shown him that the Lord loved Scruggs and had control of his life.

"Hah!" Annette said when I'd told her all that. "As if that overgrown slob would be a real Christian! He can't even wear a tie right, and he's behind in his schoolwork, and half the time he's got his pockets crammed with TNT and dynamite and things like that!"

"What's that got to do with being a Christian?" I asked.

"You just wait. I've got him all figured out. Some night he's going to dynamite Mrs. Bennett right out of her bed when she's asleep."

"Annette!"

"Oh, I've got him figured out all right. You just wait and see!"

"That's ridiculous. Scruggs is always carrying chemicals around with him because he likes science, that's all!"

"But it's always explosives!"

"It isn't always explosives," I told her. "We just hear about the explosives when they go off by accident."

"Accident, huh! Vandalism, more likely."

That was the end of that. I stopped trying to hang around with Annette. It's like trying to reason with a record playing with no "off" button.

Ticktock

So I was pretty glum. Renee, Freddy, and Marie, the three youngest kids in our family, got all excited when I took them to the park, and that was kind of nice for a while. But the park couldn't stay interesting forever.

At last one day when I was coming home from the quick mart, I saw a pickup truck in our driveway. It had a high fiber glass top on it, and overall it looked pretty beat up. I went inside the house by way of the kitchen door, put the milk I'd bought into the refrigerator, and stood undecided at the sound of voices coming from the living room.

I didn't really feel like meeting new people and getting roped into a long grown-up conversation. I decided just to go back outside again and see if Mom would call me in.

So I did. I went back outside and sat against the back bumper of the pickup truck.

I craned my neck around, watching the front door of the house. A small, fat robin hopped around on the driveway in search of gravel. A slight breeze whirled around, and the sweet smell of hay wafted out of the dark bed of the pickup.

I was just thinking that it must be a farm truck, when there was a definite rustle by my ear and a long, slim nose pushed at my cheek.

"Yugh!" I jumped back. Something lying inside the truck had come to life.

For a minute I stared at it, and it stared at me, dark eyes bright on either side of its face, lips set in a half-smile.

I stepped closer, and its nostrils worked a little bit, trying to get wind of me.

"Are you a camel?" I asked. Camels could bite, so I felt a little hesitant about putting my hand out to it. But it stretched its long neck out to me, and I saw that it was woolly. It had a white and black coat.

"A llama?" I asked. "Is that what you are?"

I did hold my hand out to it, and it sniffed at it and then at my arm. It looked me square in the face, its nose wrinkling and its eyes sparkling. Its banana-shaped ears perked forward in curiosity.

"H-hi," I said. I reached out my hand and rubbed its neck. It inspected the collar of my blouse, my buttons, and my wristwatch.

It didn't like its head to be petted, but it did like its neck scratched. But scratching a llama's woolly neck is kind of like trying to get your fingers through a shag rug. I had to stop and rest after a few minutes.

Ears forward, it gazed at the lawn, the driveway, the trees, and the street.

"Ah, so you've met!" someone called. The llama leaned out to watch the people coming toward us.

My mom was the last one out the door. She was led by a man and his wife, both wearing work clothes, both about my mom's age.

"Her name is Ticktock," the man called.

"Is she a llama?" I asked.

"Yes. North American stock, bred from a line of fine llamas." He ran his hand up Ticktock's neck, and she nosed at his shirt pockets. The woman, meanwhile, had a light halter in her hand. She gently slipped it over the llama's nose and fastened it behind its head.

"We were just going to take her for a walk," she told me. "Ticktock could stand in the truck, but she doesn't. So we have to get out and lead her every few hours."

The man took down the tailgate. The woman attached a lead to the halter. At her slight tug, Ticktock unfolded her legs, stood up, and jumped down out of the truck.

Nose wrinkling, she looked around at house and yard and gracefully followed the woman across the driveway to the grass.

"Penny, these are the Ericsons," my mom said, "Dr. and Mrs."

Dr. Ericson shook my hand. "Friend of your father," he said. "Knew him in med school before I opted out into a different field—veterinary medicine."

"Nice to meet you," I told him.

"My wife and I are just back in Wisconsin," he told me. "I was eager to see your father again and meet the family."

"You might want to set the table for lunch," Mom said. "The Ericsons will be eating with us."

I went to do as she said and to round up the little kids from the sandbox in the back yard.

I wondered why in the world the Ericsons would own a llama, but—like folks say—it's a free country.

When Freddy, Renee, and Marie came scrambling to the front of the house with me to see the llama, they all squeaked and stayed in the doorway. Ticktock looked at them, nose wrinkling back and forth in curiosity. Then she bent her neck to inspect the grass.

Freddy and Renee, both seven, had seen pictures of llamas and had read about the Pushme-Pullyou. They at last were persuaded to come out and pet the llama. But Marie, the youngest, stayed where she was.

Dad came home a few minutes later, and after Mrs. Ericson had introduced him to Ticktock, she put the llama back in the truck.

The first thing Dad and Dr. Ericson did was catch up on old news. Then Dr. Ericson got onto the topic of llamas. He told Dad that he owned a herd of forty or so.

"Forty!" Dad exclaimed. "But why? What does a man do with forty llamas?"

"Stays busy, for one thing," Dr. Ericson said. "And works on increasing his herd, like any cattle farmer."

"But for what?" Dad asked. "Their wool?"

"Maybe, except there's not much demand for it yet in the U.S."

"Well, what, then?"

"To sell as pack animals in places like Tennessee, Colorado, and California. And to sell as pets, too. They're on the upswing as exotic pets. A llama is gentle as a lamb, smart as a hound dog, funny as a kitten. And pretty clean, too."

"Expensive?" Mom asked.

"Quite expensive, although they're cheap to take care of. We paid eight thousand dollars for Ticktock, though it is possible every now and then to snap up a female for a thousand or so."

Dad whistled. "So this is a lifelong investment for you, huh?"

"Yup. Being a vet, I got a grant that helps me out financially because I can do studies on the llamas we raise. And Kate and I found a suitable tract of land that we purchased for a song."

"I hope you saw the land before you bought it," Dad said.

"Oh sure, we've been living on it for two months now. We've got barns up and a few sheds, although there's still a lot to be done to the place. It used to be a campground. It's an island on Winneca Lake, upstate about two hours."

"Hmm, and it was cheap, eh? That's odd."

"Anyway," Dr. Ericson added, "I can qualify for another grant by making the farm an educational facility. That means that—ultimately—we'll bus school children onto it for tours and produce videotapes for other llama farmers. Right now it means I need to bring some young people up and educate them about farm life."

"I think I'm catching your drift," Dad said.

"And besides that, I need a few extra hands on weekends: Friday nights and Saturdays. I can pay any kids who work for me." Dr. Ericson glanced at me.

I glanced at Dad.

Dad shrugged. "All we have right now is Penny. Jack will be back—"

"Well, I'll take what you've got right now," Dr. Ericson said with a laugh. "She seems good with animals. What do you say, Penny? Would you like to try a hand at farm work? It's hard."

"I don't mind the hard part," I told him. "Could I, Dad?"

"We'll have to see," Dad said. "We could all drive up this Saturday and pay you a visit; how's that?"

Dr. Ericson nodded, and Dad added, "Penny can bring her suitcase. If she likes the farm, she can stay and work."

Chapter Two
Everything All at Once

On Thursday night we got a call from my Uncle Justin. He said that they were on their way back from the Yukon expedition. That meant Jack and Scruggs would be coming home tomorrow.

"Now Jack can work on the farm, too!" I exclaimed to my mom.

"The Ericsons will certainly want him," Mom agreed. "But Jack might be worn out by the time he gets here."

"Just let him get a look at a llama," I said.

We were clearing up from supper when I said this. Dad looked up with a grin. "I think you're right. And maybe the Ericsons would want Scruggs along, too."

"If we could talk him into it," Mom added, with a glance at Dad.

"We'll see," Dad said. "From what Uncle Justin said on the phone, it sounds like Jack and Scruggs are good friends now. And don't forget, Scruggs likes odd animals. The llamas might charm him."

"You know, Dad, Scruggs hates to be away from Mrs. Bennett," I told him. "I think it's kind of weird that such a tough guy could be such a baby about leaving home a few weeks for the Yukon."

"Scruggs isn't a baby, Penny," Dad told me. "Now that Scruggs has a real home, he hates to be anywhere else, and that's normal. Once he gets used to the idea that his new home isn't going anyplace, he'll be ready to go out on his own."

"Do you think he'll be ready by Saturday?"

"I don't know about that."

"Besides, you may want Jack to yourself awhile," Mom told me.

"That's so," Dad agreed.

Jack really is about my best friend, even if he is a year younger than I am. He plays hockey with the guys, and in the school yard there are kids he hangs around with—just like I play girls' volleyball and have school friends. But for important things, Jack and I are partners, and we always have been. Out of school he plays catch with me a lot, and we go places on our bikes together. Maybe Mom was right.

My Uncle Justin must have called the newspapers, because some reporters showed up the next night to get a story on the Yukon trip. Not many expeditions start out from Peabody, and so it was big news.

Pastor had come over for a late supper at Dad's invitation, and so did Mrs. Bennett.

The rented car pulled in about 6:30, horn blowing and lights flashing. We all ran out to meet them. Uncle Justin jumped out of the front seat, and Jack and Scruggs hopped out of the back.

Scruggs, of course, went right to Mrs. Bennett, and Jack said "cheese" for the newspaper photographer and then hugged Mom and Dad. The three little kids were jumping up and down and yelling for Jack.

At last he got through to me and surprised me by giving me a box of candy wrapped up with a real walrus tusk (the label said).

"Hey, thanks!" I exclaimed.

"You're welcome," he told me. "You get to have the next adventure. I'm ready to sit one out."

"Not when you hear what I have to tell you," I said.

Jack looked at me a little sharply, and I grinned.

"Will there be room for Scruggs?" he asked. "On this adventure, I mean?"

I was a little surprised at how quick he was to want to include Scruggs, but I said, "Sure, but he hates adventures."

"Not anymore. He's cured," Jack promised. "We had a great time. So tell me, what's the new adventure all about? Say, what's for supper? I'm starved."

The reporter and photographer were clamoring around Uncle Justin, and Pastor was talking to Scruggs and Mrs. Bennett. Mom was trying to get everybody inside to eat.

"Llamas," I said to Jack.

"Lima beans? Yuck. I was hoping for roast beef or—"

"No, llamas, llamas. Two-L llamas!"

"Two-L-llamas? What's a two-L-llama?"

"You know, long neck, woolly coat, and long ears?"

His eyes popped. "We're eating llamas? For dinner?"

"No, you mug. That's the adventure. Llamas!"

"Like in *Amy Belle and the Secret in Peru?*" he asked.

I used to read this mystery series called *The Amy Belle Mystery Books*. Jack always made fun of it, but every now and then he says something that makes me suspect he read them as much as I did.

"How'd you know about that book?" I asked him. "How'd you know there were llamas in it?"

"There was a llama on the cover. When I first saw it, I thought it was Amy Belle, but she's not that pretty."

"That is *not* nice," I told him.

"Actually, the ears tipped me off. Amy Belle keeps hers tied down with her titian hair in a pink scarf—"

"You *have* read those books!" I cried.

"What's this about llamas?" he asked. "Are we going to Peru?"

"No. Winneca Lake, Wisconsin."

"Where do the llamas come in?"

"They live there. Forty of them. And their owners need some farmhands. I'll explain it to you after dinner."

Chapter Three
Welcome to Winneca Farms

Because the Ericsons wanted us to bring as many people as we could on Saturday, Dad invited Scruggs and Mrs. Bennett along. It took quite a bit of work to get everybody into the station wagon, what with Marie wanting to sit next to Mom, Scruggs wanting to sit next to Mrs. Bennett, and Jack wanting to sit next to Scruggs.

I ended up in the back with Freddy and Renee. I was a little bit mad at Jack. He acted like Scruggs was his hero or something and I was just his dopey sister. But I knew I would have the last laugh. Jack's suitcase was right next to mine in the luggage compartment. It hadn't taken him long to decide that he wanted to work on the llama farm, too. But Scruggs had said no. So I'd get Jack to myself after all.

It took about two hours to get to Winneca Lake. It was a fairly big lake, set in hilly country. The highway ran pretty close to its shore, and there were houses here and there. Every now and then we'd pass a house built right on the shore, with a pier at its back porch and a couple of boats moored. Then we passed a big billboard that said, "Winneca Lake: Where Bass Reign." And it had a picture of a fisherman in waders bringing in a bass, and there were other bass flip-flopping out of the water all around him "as if they were in an earthquake," Jack said.

The town of Winneca was made up of about a dozen streets and some alleys. We just skirted it on our way around the lake. We crossed a steel bridge that spanned a marsh and followed the highway back up the other side of the lake.

At last Dad turned down a narrow dirt road that disappeared into some trees. We followed it down a steep bank, across a causeway, and up another bank. A small white sign by the roadside read "Winneca Farms." "Where Llamas Reign!" Jack cried. We went through an open wooden gate that had been hog-wired and followed the road out from under the shady trees. Dad drove past what looked like an L-shaped bunkhouse and then stopped in front of a worn-looking house.

"This must be the farmhouse," he guessed. "Seems like some of these buildings are left over from the old camp, I suppose."

"There's new barns down there," Scruggs said, pointing back the way we'd come to a couple of huge red barns. They were obviously new, with fresh white trim. There was a red and white tractor shed farther up on our right.

We piled out of the car in time to see Dr. Ericson come up from the tractor shed. He waved.

Out past the shed were the pastures. The nearer ones looked pretty scruffy and worn down, without much grass, except along the sides.

Jack squinted and said, "This place used to be a camp, huh? Look at that pasture, Scruggs. It's hard to tell with that shed in the way, but I think that pasture used to be the camp's baseball diamond!"

I felt annoyed. "Oh, come on, it's just a bare hunk of land."

"No, he's right," Scruggs said. "It isn't a perfect diamond, but it looks like you could put the white lines down with no problem. Reminds me of the ball field at home in the spring before the Little League has it limed."

"Would you guys quit playing junior detective?" I asked.

Jack glanced quickly at me, hurt, and Scruggs cocked an eyebrow.

"Penny," Mom said. "That wasn't nice."

"Well, it doesn't look like a ball diamond to me," I said and put my head down.

"Hi, folks!" Dr. Ericson called. He thrust his hand out to Dad. "Nice to have you here. Come on up to the house."

The farmhouse was old and sturdy. A lot of the doors creaked, and a faint smell of ham—or perhaps sausage—lingered with the seasoned old smell of wood fires that had burned over the years in the great fireplace. Our many footsteps echoed on the hard brown floors.

The kitchen was spacious and had a huge trestle table at one end, where Mrs. Ericson was fixing the sloppy joes and fried potatoes we were going to have for lunch. Jack took one look at the food and said that this was the place for him. He seemed about ready to forgive me for calling him a junior detective.

At that point Dr. Ericson started talking to Scruggs to get him to change his mind.

"I really do need kids up here," he told Scruggs. "That's why, I'm willing to drive all the way down to Peabody and back every Friday and Saturday. I need that grant to keep this place going. And think how great it would sound to tell your friends you've worked on a llama farm."

"Well, I guess I could," Scruggs admitted. "Maybe in about a week or so."

Jack beamed. My heart sank.

"And Jean could, too," Scruggs added. "I mean, if you still need more kids."

Dr. Ericson nodded at that. Jack's eyes got big in horror. "What? Jean?" he asked.

"Say," Dad said, "that sounds like a fine idea. She'll be home in a couple of weeks."

Jean was the perfect child. Straight *A*'s. No cavities. No imagination, either, but people rarely grade you on imagination.

"She's too young," Jack sputtered. "She's only eleven!"

"Why, from what my mother says, Jean's already riding horses and helping on your uncle's farm," Scruggs said. "She'd be all broke in for llama farming."

"Sounds wonderful!" Dr. Ericson exclaimed.

"We should have thought of it ourselves," Dad agreed. "She just loves her uncle's farm."

Jack and I glanced at each other helplessly. I didn't mind so much. After Jack had gone to the Yukon, I'd gotten to like Jean a little more. Sure, she was too wishy-washy and a little bit of a chicken. But otherwise she was okay. She was a lot better to hang around with than Annette. I wondered if Scruggs was going to volunteer Annette, too. But he didn't.

"Looks like there's a car out there," Dr. Ericson said. "I'd better go see who it is."

He hurried out, and Mrs. Bennett redirected the conversation into other channels.

Jack glanced at me, chagrined and puzzled. He didn't want our little sister tagging along. Like I said, I wasn't especially enthusiastic about it either, but it was kind of nice to see Jack squirm after the way he'd been acting toward me. While everyone else got to talking about llamas, Jack whispered under his breath, "At least I get to bunk with Scruggs, and you'll get stuck with Jean."

I hadn't thought of that.

Chapter Four
First Troubles

"Penny, honey, run out and ask my husband and his company to come in, would you?" Mrs. Ericson asked. "Lunch is all ready, and there's plenty more for company."

I said yes and ran to get Dr. Ericson. I came running down the front steps just in time to hear the sound of his voice. He was very angry. The stranger stood beside a dark blue car that was kind of official-looking. He was a young man with a suit and tie and dark glasses.

"And I'm telling you to get off my land," Dr. Ericson was saying as I ran up. "No two-bit piece of bureaucracy's going to close this farm—"

"I've told you, it isn't to close your farm, just to get an accurate count."

"You know perfectly well this farm's got to have more than forty head on it to make money," he roared at the stranger. "We'll be running fifty to sixty head if we can, and the land will support them."

The younger man tried again. "But the county ordinances—"

19

"Hang the county ordinances!" Dr. Ericson cried. "I applied for and received a license to bring forty llamas onto this land, and you aren't going to touch this land or those llamas until I see a court order. Now get going!"

At the sight of me, they both stopped and glanced up sharply. Then the stranger walked to his car and got in, slamming the door. He pulled out quickly and drove away.

"Is something wrong, Dr. Ericson?" I asked.

"County ordinance!" he exclaimed. "That fella says this land is zoned for only one grazing animal per acre. And according to the books, this island is only thirty-five acres. So we're over by five head."

"Was he trying to close it down?" I asked.

"No, not yet. He says he wants to bring out a team of surveyors to remeasure the land and its grazing acreage and make a recommendation to the county commissioners. I told him that until he could show me a court order authorizing him to do that, he'd better never set foot on this farm again."

"But—" I began. Then, remembering how angry he'd been, I hesitated.

"What?" he asked.

"I mean, won't you have to let them survey it? If it's illegal to—"

"It's not illegal!" he said. "Penny, I sent letters to the county commissioners and the township, announcing my plans, and they gave me the go-ahead. Then some young puppy unearths an old law directed at sheep and cattle raisers. And he wants to survey my land and make his recommendation. What does he know about llamas?" he demanded. "This is between me and the county commissioners, if they have a problem with my llamas.

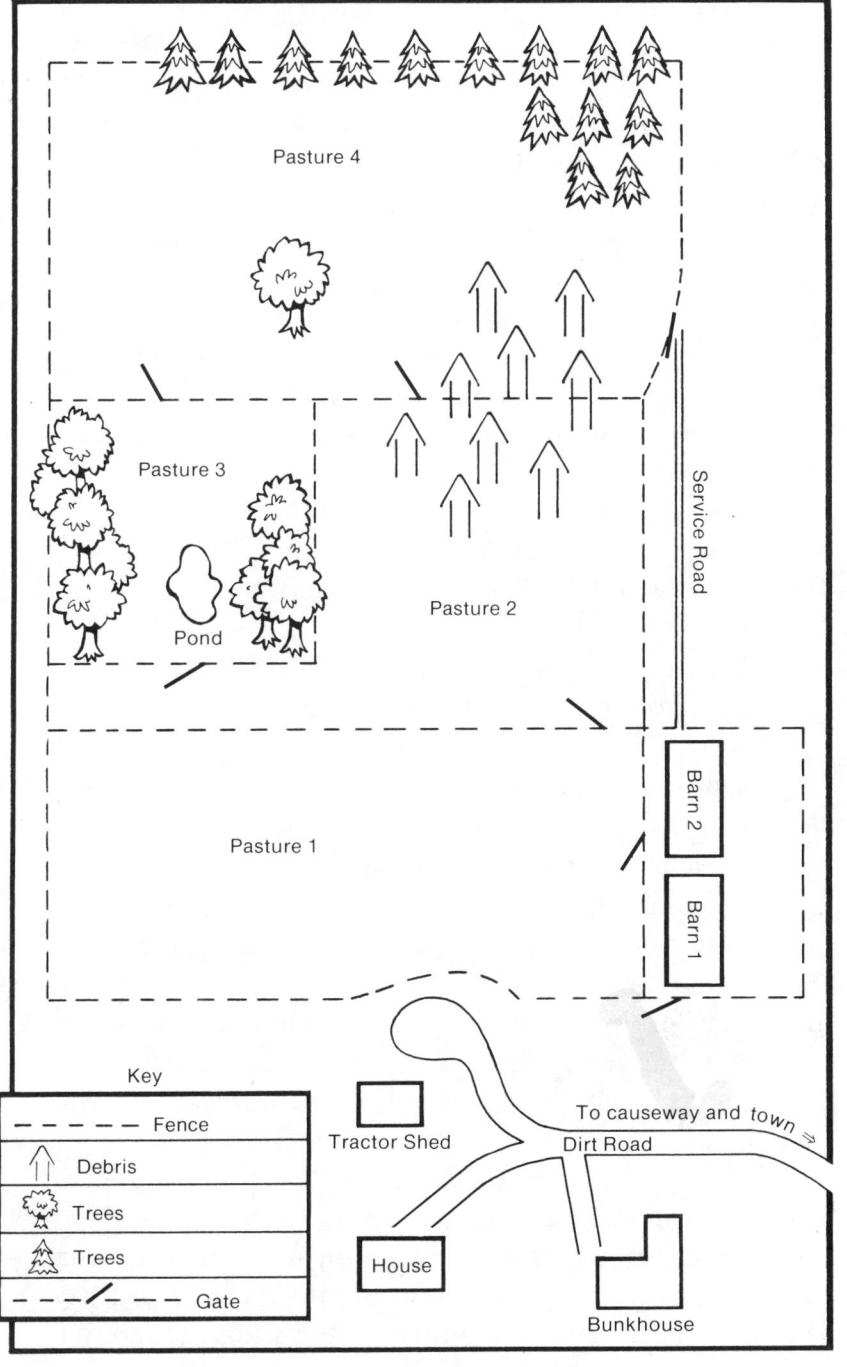

But I told them how big my herd would have to be, and I showed them that decent pasturage will support four llamas to the acre. I won't be run off or scared into submission by some kid just out of college who doesn't understand the first thing about farming."

We went inside on that, and Dr. Ericson told everyone about his unwelcome visitor.

When he'd finished, Dad said, "You were wise not to let him make a survey of the island, Bud. If there should prove to be any type of legal dispute, the land ought to be surveyed by a neutral third party who has the consent of both you and the commissioners."

"What I can't understand," Mom said, "is why everyone would let you move in and build and then check the books for such an ordinance."

"Unless," Scruggs guessed, "someone was looking for an excuse to cause trouble for the farm."

"Now, Scruggs—" Dad began.

"But listen, Mr. Derwood," he said. "When the state government or county government tries to close down private schools, don't they usually do it by hunting up old laws and regulations?"

"Well, yes, that very often is true," Dad agreed. "But why would anyone want to close the farm?" He glanced at Dr. Ericson. "I think it's more likely that you've run into a young man who wants to move ahead in county politics. He's got every regulation memorized and will be pushing to whip everyone into line."

"Well, if trouble comes of it," Dr. Ericson added, "I can explain to a judge that I was granted a permit for the farm despite the regulation and prove to him that thirty-five acres can easily support a herd of forty llamas and all their offspring. If the judge orders me

First Troubles

to limit the herd or move, I'll appeal. Somebody will certainly see the difference between raising llamas and raising cattle or sheep."

"And of course, we'll pray for the judges to be fair," Mrs. Bennett added.

Dad glanced at Dr. Ericson, who only said, "Well, every little bit helps."

Everyone began to talk about more cheerful things. I kept thinking about Dr. Ericson's anger, and how he'd called the man from the county names—I guess a Christian *could* do those things. I mean, I know Christians aren't perfect—but he'd never yet referred to God, nothing at all. Mom and Dad—whenever they got into conversations—would usually mention things like the Lord getting Jack back safely from the Yukon, or providing a good vacation for Jean in Alabama, or even smaller things like keeping us all safe on the road. But the Ericsons never mentioned God, as though they weren't aware of Him at all.

After lunch, we went outside to tour the farm, and I got Dad by himself. We trailed a little behind the others.

"Dad," I asked, "are the Ericsons saved?"

He smiled a little, approving of my interest. "No, I'm afraid not, Penny. I've witnessed to Bud, and he says he believes in God, but he doesn't really believe that he's a sinner." He put his arm across my shoulders. "When you grow up, Pen, you're going to have to work among people who don't believe what we believe. One reason I want you to work here is for you to learn to respect and love unconverted people and always be a witness to them of God's love and mercy. Sometimes it's easy, and sometimes it's hard."

Chapter Five
Settling In

It hadn't taken long for Jack and me to decide that we were sure we wanted to work on the llama farm. Since school hadn't started yet, we could spend the whole next week there.

"What I'd like to know," Jack said as we sat on the porch of the bunkhouse and watched the family car disappear down the dirt road, "is what put it into Scruggs's head to include Jean."

"You've got me," I told him.

He put his chin on his hand and gazed into the distance at the barns and the trees behind them. Supposedly we were putting our gear into our separate rooms. The Ericsons had given us an hour to get settled in and report back for dinner. It had taken us fifteen minutes.

"Well, it'll be a couple weeks until she gets back," he said. "Who knows? Maybe she won't want to come. Jean likes books a lot more than action. Has she read all your old Amy Belle books yet? How about *Mystery in the Moosehead Factory?* Maybe we could get her started on it, and she won't want to come."

"I'm not sure I have that one," I told him.

"How about this one?" He put up a hand, and his eyes got a faraway look in them. "Amy Belle quickly ran a brush through her auburn hair until it shone. Her widowed father, the wealthy businessman Lethbridge Belle, would be coming in soon on his private jet. His latest telegram had been brief but urgent. He had to speak to her about some new mystery that had him baffled. Vast fortunes and entire governments might be at stake.

"Outside, she could hear the engine of her jaunty sports car rev up as Phil Philmont tuned it up for her. Other than Amy's anxieties about international finance and world politics, the town of Cranberry Heights was quiet that Saturday morning."

Jack turned, grinned at me, and then bowed.

"That's great! I almost forgot about that one!" I told him. "Which book begins that way?"

"Let's see, *Mystery in the Moosehead Factory* and *The Moon Surface Oil Rig Caper* and *The Treasure in the Attic of the Old House on the Deserted Street*."

"It's odd how those stories always get jumbled in my mind," I told him. "And I usually remember good stories."

"This still doesn't solve our problems," he said.

I shrugged. "Guess we'll have to wait and see if she comes."

The Ericsons had already shown us the pastures and the llamas. There were four fenced pastures on the farm, and they were strung out in order, 1-2-3-4. Pasture 1 had been the ball diamond, and it was closest to the house and barns. Pasture 2 was covered with high, rough grass and lots of debris from the old camp buildings.

Settling In

Pasture 3 was a tiny square pasture cut into Pasture 2. It had lots of trees and a pond and was called the Nursery. Dr. Ericson planned to keep the mothers and young llamas—called *crias*—there. Pasture 4 was planted with fescue, but it needed to be replanted in places, and parts of it still needed to be cleared. There was a lot of deadwood, old stumps, and a fringe of trees up on one corner of it. Beyond Pasture 4 was a wooded strip and then the lake shore.

The llamas generally hung around Pasture 1, because that was where they got fed and had their water trough.

They were usually free to walk wherever they wanted to in any of the pastures, except for Pasture 3, the Nursery, where the crias and their mothers spent their days. That was closed off. But Doc Ericson was very careful about the security of the pastures. "I don't want anything bigger than a squirrel getting into those fields," he told us that night at supper. "Once a week someone's got to check the fences. That'll be your Friday night job."

"Wow! We'll ride the fences like cowboys," Jack said.

"Except you'll have to walk," he told us. "No horses."

"No six-guns, either," I added.

"That reminds me," Dr. Ericson said, "I do have a gun rack here, locked, of course. Can you two shoot?"

"We both took a gun safety course with our dad," I told him. "But Jack's a better shot."

"Well, we might go out and practice a little," he said. "There's only a slight chance of some wild animal breaking into the pasture, but it's best to be prepared for anything. If you hear the dinner gong ringing and see the floodlights come on at night, run for the house and be ready for an emergency."

Jack and I must have looked pretty serious at that, and Dr. Ericson laughed. "Don't worry, kids. There never has been an emergency out here. I doubt we'll ever have one."

Chapter Six
An Emergency

Doc Ericson had to make our visit educational so he could qualify for a research grant, and during that week he taught us a lot about the history of llamas in the U.S. We also learned how to groom them and how to mix their feed.

There were forty llamas in all, thirty-four adults and six crias. There was one special male, Jock, who was boss of the herd. He took charge of all the females and every now and then had a spit-fight with the two other yearling males to remind them who was boss. Male llamas do have fangs to bite with, and if they get in a real fight, you'll see them leap up and come down on each other, biting, slashing with their hooves, trying to knock each other down, and spitting quarts at each other. But usually the lead male only has to let loose a couple of pints of spit at the other males to let them know he's still in charge.

Since female llamas don't have any upper teeth, their number one defense is to spit. And when a llama spits at you, you can consider yourself—in no uncertain terms—spit upon. They can reach right down into their stomachs to spit, unlike people, who use only their throats.

So in a sense, llamas are pretty well defended. They can sense intruders at a distance, and they will instinctively aim for an attacker's face to spit at, in order to blind him.

On the other hand, if a llama senses an approaching attacker but is trapped in a fenced pasture, he can't get away. And a llama under attack by more than one creature is pretty helpless. Two medium-sized dogs can pull down a full-grown llama. That was why Dr. Ericson had the whole place hog-wired.

Supposedly we also learned how to halter a llama, if you want to count it that way. What actually happened was that Jack got his arms 'round Ticktock's neck, and she bucked him all over the barnyard for about ten minutes. Then, when she was exhausted and wanted a drink, I got the harness around her nose and Jack fastened it before she could buck again.

"If we were taller and heavier, we could do it," Jack said. "But I can hardly reach her nose unless she keeps her head down."

"Look, two of us ought to be smarter than one of her," I told him. "Size has nothing to do with it. Even the trainer's manual says that."

"Well, I wish Ticktock would read the manual, then." But at the challenge in my words, he came up to Ticktock again and got his arms around her neck to get her halter off. We were in the barnyard. Ticktock had been nibbling up some spilled grain. She took one look at Jack and started jumping again, taking him with her.

His legs swung up one way and then the other as she jumped and turned and bucked.

An Emergency

"All I want to do is get your halter off!" he yelled.

"She must think it's a game!" I called as I chased them around, trying to get a way to jump in and grab her 'round the neck on the other side.

"Sure it's a game—Kill the Kid!" Jack yelled. "Would you do something?" But Ticktock turned away and jumped. I saw Jack's legs swing out past her. He tried to get his footing to brace himself. "Penny!" he called. I shut my eyes and jumped in.

Ticktock snorted indignantly, as though she thought I was cheating. "Quick! The buckle's on your side," I said. A second later the halter came off. Ticktock stopped and stood stock-still.

"She does think it's a game!" Jack exclaimed. We let the tired llama go back to the pasture. "Boy," Jack said. "I'm glad Doc gets the grant just for teaching us. Because if it depended on how much we learned, I'm not sure he'd get enough to cover postage."

Of course, along with the fun stuff, we also "learned" to pick up rocks in the pasture, scrape paint on the outside of the bunkhouse, and weed the garden in the front of the house. In fact, most of what we did was just plain old work, but it was nice to have Jack there to talk to.

On our second Saturday we hurried to get the chores done early so that we could leave for home right after lunch.

"Now, you two be sure to bring Scruggs with you next Friday," Mrs. Ericson said as we sat down to eat. "We certainly can use him."

"Sure!" Jack exclaimed. I only nodded.

"And your sister Jean, too," Doc Ericson added.

Llamas on the Loose

Jack hesitated, looking glum, and I said, "She's not back from Alabama yet."

"Maybe next time then," Mrs. Ericson said. "Be nice to have two boys and two girls, because then nobody gets picked on and nobody gets left out."

Well, it was obvious that she didn't know Jean. Jean was just born with the tendency to get picked on and left out. I sighed heavily.

"You two eat up," Doc Ericson told us as he stood up. "I want to get the crias out to the Nursery before we leave for Peabody. The yearling males are too rough with them."

We nodded and he went out. A minute later the dinner gong that hung on the porch started banging furiously.

Jack and I looked at each other and we both said, "Trouble!" at the same time before we rushed out. Mrs. Ericson followed.

"Look! Look!" Dr. Ericson cried as we all came bursting out the door. We looked. Everything was silent. A faint breeze kicked up dust in Pasture 1.

"Everything seems quiet," Jack said.

"*Seems* quiet!" Dr. Ericson exclaimed. "The llamas are gone! Gone!"

We ran down the steps.

"The gate's open," I said and pointed at the wide pasture gate. Mrs. Ericson squinted and said, "The gate to Pasture 2 is open, too."

Dr. Ericson ran back into the house and came out with his field glasses. He used them to sweep over the pastures. "All the gates are open! Quick, get in the truck!"

An Emergency

We scrambled for the pickup. Jack and I hopped into the truck-bed, and the Ericsons got into the front. With a mighty jerk of the gears, we took off.

Pasture 1 had the gate most often used as an exit gate. By that I mean that Pasture 4's gate led into the pasture alongside it. Pasture 3's gate led into Pasture 2, and Pasture 2's gate led into Pasture 1. But Pasture 1 had a gate that opened into the barnyard, and the barnyard gate opened to the dirt road. There was an exit gate on the far side of Pasture 4, but we never used it much because it was so far from the barns, and I'm not sure the llamas even knew it was there.

We jolted down that dirt road, headed for the causeway. A welcome sight met us as we came down the bank.

The llamas stood on either side of the causeway, knee-deep in shallow lake water. Most of them ignored us. They were busy drinking or browsing at some of the plants on the banks or lifting their muzzles to catch the smells. The two yearling males were having a spit fight. Mrs. Ericson hopped out of the cab and Jack jumped out of the back. I started to follow, but Dr. Ericson yelled, "I'll get the sheriff!" and took off again before I could get out.

Jack and Mrs. Ericson nodded and waved. I don't think Doc Ericson knew I was still in the truck until we pulled into town. But he was so flustered at the llamas having been let out that he simply parked and said, "I'll get the sheriff!"

And he rushed up the sidewalk.

I felt kind of blank myself. I hopped out of the truck and looked around.

Winneca certainly wasn't a big or a busy town. Right across the street was a big warehouse-type building that said "Ernie's Everything Outlet" on it. Instead of regular doors like any other store, it had huge garage doors that opened onto the street. The effect was that the whole front of the store seemed to be opened for the public to walk in and out. But at the moment nobody was walking out of Ernie's Everything Outlet. Instead, a huge crowd seemed to be pushing to get in. Somebody was yelling, "Stay back, folks! It may bite!" That was why the crowd couldn't get in.

I walked across the street in time to hear someone say, "Looks like a Shetland pony to me."

"It's a baby camel, I tell you."

I started to get a sinking feeling. I pushed through the crowd to where the store manager was keeping everyone back.

The inside of the store was vast and cluttered. A pile of baskets lay here, a bundle of blankets there. Crates and cartons had been stacked to make aisles, and there was a candy center. There were crates of boxed candy all stacked together and several open bins of penny candy under a sign that said, "Take Your Pick, Penny Candy only $1.00 a pound."

And there, with her muzzle buried in the black licorice bits, was Ticktock. She lifted her head and looked over at me.

I'm not sure that Ticktock actually ate any of the licorice, but I think the pungent smell must have fascinated her. She put her muzzle back into the bin.

"Mister," I said. "I know that llama."

"Is it yours?" the manager asked me.

An Emergency

"Well no, but I'm a friend of the family, you might say."

"Can you get it out of here?" he asked.

"If you've got a rope," I told him.

"This is a store!" he exclaimed. "What would we do with rope?"

"The sign says it's an everything store."

"Everything but rope," he told me.

"How about a dog leash?" I asked.

"Ninety-nine cents and it's yours."

"I don't have ninety-nine cents," I told him. "And I only want to borrow it."

He went and found a dog leash. I tied a knot in it about a third of the way from the end, and walked up to Ticktock.

"That kid must be from the circus," someone guessed. "She knows how to handle a baby giraffe."

"Ticktock," I said, holding the leash behind my back. "Ticktock."

The llama looked up at me. There were black smudges on her nose.

The manager crowded up behind me. "A whole bin of candy, ruined!" he exclaimed. "Ruined by a baby giraffe!"

Ticktock put her banana ears back and raised her muzzle, eyeing him sideways.

"Stop," I said to him in a soft but urgent voice. "You're scaring her." And I halted where I was. He bumped into me.

"Scaring her!" he exclaimed. "She's eating my candy!"

"Don't!" I said as her eyes widened. "Oh no!" I covered my face with my hands and ducked.

Llamas on the Loose

Ticktock missed me when she spit, but I'm afraid she got the manager. He yelled, and she wheeled and raced up one of the aisles.

"Rabies! It's got rabies!" he yelled.

I ran after her.

She wasn't in sports shoes or baby clothes. I decided to look at the food aisles, and I soon found them.

A scream from the back of the store led me to her.

The wholesale flowers were back there. One lady—a customer—rushed past me, but when I got there I saw the florist lady nervously holding out a bouquet to Ticktock. The llama gently sniffed along the tops of the carnations and took a nibble of baby's breath.

"She won't hurt you," I said. Ticktock glanced at me and went back to browsing. "Ticktock," I said, and put my free hand out to her.

She really wanted me to leave her alone, but as long as she had the flowers, she decided not to resist. I slipped my arm around her neck. While I talked to her I got the dog leash onto her neck and fastened it above the knot I had tied in it. That way the lead couldn't get too tight and choke her.

"Whew!" I said.

"Is she yours?" the florist lady asked me.

"No, I'm just her maid." And I laughed a little.

Just then Doc Ericson, the sheriff, and the store manager (who was mopping his face) came up the aisle.

Doc Ericson was so glad that Ticktock was okay that he didn't mind how much the store manager had to say to him. He paid for the licorice and the flowers. I took the bouquet, and with that and the lead, I got the llama to come with me.

Llamas on the Loose

Ticktock was as mild as milk once we got her out of the store. She gladly hopped into the pickup on command. I followed her.

Chapter Seven
Startling News

"Sounds like you two have had quite the adventure," Dad said that night when we told him all about it.

"The sheriff said he'd keep an eye on the farm," Jack told him. "Why do you think someone would let out all the llamas, Dad?"

"Seems to me that someone probably thought it would be tremendously funny," Dad said. "Either that or it was a good way to get everybody away from the house."

"That's what Doc Ericson realized later," I told Dad. "So he ran back to the house while we herded the llamas together. But nothing was messed up."

"No, nobody had been there," Jack said. "And the barns and tool shed were safe and sound, too."

"Hmmm." Dad looked at his coffee cup. We were at the dining room table. Freddy, Renee, and Marie were in the kitchen with Mom, helping her get dessert. They liked to do that to make sure they got the big pieces.

A moment later they trooped in, each bearing two plates of pie. When it was all passed around, Mom said,

"Well, we'll be driving down to Alabama to pick Jean up next Friday. I guess I'd better get you two to the store for school clothes this week. I don't know when I'll have time to shop for Jean if she's going to be on the farm every weekend."

"Hmm, maybe she shouldn't go to the farm for a couple of weekends," Jack said, hiding his hope.

"Jean's not going to miss the fun over school clothes," Dad said. It was a pronouncement. We didn't argue. He looked at Mom. "It won't be a crime for her not to start the first day of school in a new dress. And she'll be heartsick if we keep her here while everyone else goes to the llama farm."

"You're right," Mom said. "We can go shopping after school on the first few days."

Jack grimaced. "Are you sure she'll want to come?" he asked.

"She's in love with the farm in Alabama," Mom said. "It's been good for her, too."

"May we be excused?" Freddy asked.

"Please, please!" Renee and Marie shouted.

Dad nodded and they raced away. Jack and I stood up, and Dad said, "Hang on a second, Penny and Jack."

We glanced at each other and sat back down. Mom began to clear up the dessert dishes.

"Look," Dad said. "I wish you two would give Jean a break."

"She's younger than us!" Jack blurted.

"Jack, whenever Penny's not around, you have a good time with Jean. And Penny, the same is true of you whenever Jack isn't around. But when the two of you are together, you fall into the old routine."

Jack didn't say anything.

Startling News

"But Jean's afraid of everything," I said.

"I'm not asking you to go mountain climbing with her," Dad said. "Just include her. Don't make her feel left out at the farm."

Jack sighed.

"Okay," I told Dad. "We'll do our best."

I saw Jack glance sharply at me, as if to ask, "What do you mean, *we?*" But then he looked down again.

Dad stood up. "Jean might surprise you after all," he said. And then he walked out.

"If she can stay out of the poison ivy and not fall into the lake, she'll surprise me," Jack mumbled.

"Oh, come on, Jack," I told him. "Give it up. Scruggs is on her side, too."

"Yeah, I still want to find out why he suggested her. Let's go over to his house."

I said okay. Mom told us we could walk over; so we called him and went over.

Once upon a time Mrs. Bennett had granted Scruggs a basement laboratory. But because there'd been one too many explosions down there, she'd made him change it to his private gym. He had his weights and a full-length mirror, but he wanted to make it his study, too. Part of the room had a leftover strip of carpet on the floor, and there was a saggy easy chair nearby. He also had a lot of boards scattered around so he could build a bookshelf.

In fact, when we came clattering down the steps, we found Scruggs bent over the boards with a hammer in his hand and some old nails in his mouth.

"Hi!" Jack called in greeting.

Scruggs looked up. "Hi!" he called back around the nails in his mouth. He spit them into his hand. "What's up?"

"You going with us next weekend?" Jack asked.

"Guess so. If it's okay."

"Sure!" Jack flopped down onto the floor and examined one of the board pieces. I took the sagging easy chair.

"Say, Scruggs," Jack asked.

"Hm?" Scruggs had a thin strip of wood—a length of a two by four—braced against the edge of a plank. It looked to me like he was trying to build a frame first for his bookcase before he nailed the other planks in place.

"Why Jean?" Jack asked.

"Why Jean what?" Scruggs asked. He glanced up at Jack and then started hammering a nail into the frame.

"Why did you ask for Jean to come to the farm?" Jack asked over the banging.

Scruggs glanced at Jack. "I thought she was into farms these days. Figured she'd get a kick out of those snooty llamas."

He went back to his hammering. Jack and I glanced at each other. Finished with one nail, Scruggs selected another, pushed his hair out of his eyes, and started hammering again.

"She likes to tag along," Jack yelled over the racket.

"I don't mind."

"She's scared of everything," I added.

He stopped his work and looked up at us. "You guys mad 'cause I wanted her to come?"

"No, we're not mad," Jack said.

Startling News

"Well, that's good, 'cause I would hate to think I got you mad." Scruggs got on hands and knees to examine his spare boards. "But the fact is, I picked on Jean so much when we were younger that she's scared of me now. She always thinks I'm going to make fun of her. Like that time I was just kidding around and I tried on her glasses." He glanced up at us. "She was ready to cry, you know?"

He went back to his boards. "That's when I decided to make things up to her. I promised God I'd be nice to Jean. Don't you guys think she needs confidence?" He looked at us again. "I think if she had more confidence she'd get over being scared. And she'd be able to take a joke better. Rats. None of these boards will fit. Well, I guess it's getting kind of late, anyway."

Jack and I had to agree with him. We were pretty tired after the week's hard work and all the excitement this afternoon.

In fact, I was still sleepy the next morning when I got to Sunday school. I would have sat there and yawned through the whole hour, but then our teacher started asking questions that made us think, and that woke me up for a while.

After Sunday, the week sort of dragged until Friday came again. That was when Mom and Dad and the little kids left to go pick up Jean. Doc Ericson came and picked up Scruggs, Jack, and me to go to the farm.

"Anything new?" Jack asked him right away.

"No news is good news," he told us. "And there's no news except that you and Penny have to check the fences when we get there."

"Oh, I'll take Scruggs instead," Jack said.

I opened my mouth and then closed it again. Here we go again, I thought. It was the same routine as before: Jack forgot all about me as soon as he got around Scruggs.

"Sheriff's coming up tonight," Doc told us. "Going to have supper with us."

"Has he got any clues on who let the llamas go?" Jack asked.

"Nary a one. I think it's just a social call."

By the time we got to the farm, it was almost suppertime. Jack and Scruggs waited long enough to toss Scruggs's gear into their room in the bunkhouse, and then they went out to inspect the fences. I went to say hello to the llamas and help with the night feeding for the mothers.

Llamas love to be admired, and they're so curious that they like to come and sniff at your gloves and buttons and whatever you're carrying. But as a general rule they really don't like to be petted. Ticktock, however, was an exception.

She came right up to me, holding her head cocked to the side a little so that I'd know to scratch her neck for her. Her previous owner had trained her to be affectionate. I felt better when she welcomed me that way. I scratched her neck and let her inspect me.

Then I went into the barn to get the buckets. It didn't take long to give the new mothers their grain mix. Just as I was coming back to the barn, I saw the sheriff pull up.

After I put the buckets away, I went up to the house to help Mrs. Ericson. Sheriff Duncan and Doc Ericson were talking in the living room. Just as we got the food set out, Jack and Scruggs came in.

Startling News

We all sat down to fried chicken, coleslaw, potato salad, and iced tea. The Ericsons didn't pray before they ate, and so Jack and I hadn't been, either. But when Doc Ericson said, "Well, let's start," Scruggs bowed his head.

Everybody looked at him, and then Scruggs looked up. "Oh," he said. "Excuse me. I thought you meant to say the blessing."

The sheriff had his hand on a chicken leg, but he put it down. "Sure," he said.

"Well, uh, why don't you ask it, Scruggs?" Mrs. Ericson said.

"Oh, sure," and so he bowed his head and said grace. After he finished, Jack and I shot guilty looks at each other. We'd never even suggested it. As we passed the food around, I handed Jack the meat and whispered, "That's not the only chicken in this room."

He rolled his eyes at the joke but gave me a look as if to agree with me.

Sheriff Duncan dug into the potato salad. Between mouthfuls he said, "No leads on what happened out here last week."

"Been quiet since then," Doc observed.

"Yeah, all that about bad luck and jinxes is just stuff to scare kids with."

Jack, Scruggs, and I looked up at him and stopped eating.

"Hmmm," Doc said, taking a forkful of coleslaw.

"You know," Sheriff said. "What with the flood and all that. Some folks said no good would come of it."

Doc looked up at him. "What are you talking about?"

Sheriff Duncan set down his knife and fork. "Now it just goes to show you," he said, "what the county will do to make a sale."

"What did they do?" Doc asked.

"They haven't told you about the history of this place, huh?"

"Should they have?"

"Well," Sheriff said. " 'Bout ten years ago, this was a working camp. Until we had a season of bad rains. Drainage used to be bad, and with conditions being what they were, and the camp being under poor supervision, there was a mighty bad flood."

"On the island?" Doc asked.

"Haven't you ever wondered why the debris is so bad in places?" the sheriff asked. "When it flooded, the water came rushing in and covered almost everything. Flooded on a stormy night, past midnight. Nearly destroyed the camper cabins and picked up the bunkhouse and moved it fifty yards."

"Anyone hurt?" Doc asked.

"Sure. Plenty. And four campers were killed. Drowned."

Mrs. Ericson gasped.

"That's why it came to you so cheap," the sheriff said. "Nobody else would buy it. Just stood here for years and years."

Doc threw down his napkin and stood up. "Those frauds! They never told me—"

"Now, simmer down, Doc, simmer down," the sheriff said. "It was there if you'd read the records. Nobody falsified anything."

"This island is a time bomb. It could flood again!"

Startling News

The sheriff shook his head. "No. The state's seen to that. The drainage around the lake is all taken care of. Won't flood again."

Doc sat down.

"But folks say you can't make a go of it out here," Sheriff Duncan said. "Say it's a tragic, sad place. From what I understand, the folks running the camp were a couple of negligent folks. Weren't even really qualified. Didn't know anything about safety standards or rescue procedures. In fact, they up and vanished the day after it all happened."

"That's criminal," Doc exclaimed.

Sheriff nodded. "You're right. But we've never tracked 'em down. Don't know what their game was. Couldn't a' made much running a dinky camp." He shrugged. "Anyway, some folks say the island ought to be left deserted. Naturally the county commissioners didn't look at it that way."

Doc and Mrs. Ericson looked at each other. Scruggs and Jack looked at each other. Nobody looked at me. But the news had my head in a whirl.

"And on top of that," Doc muttered, "on top of not telling me about that, they had the nerve to send some guy out here to harass me about my herd."

The sheriff looked puzzled. "Yeah, I can't seem to pin him down. He couldn't have been local. Maybe the state had him come out. Somebody might have complained about you." He afforded us a grin. "Maybe they didn't like llamas next door."

But Doc Ericson didn't laugh. "This whole business smells," he said. "Smells downright rotten!"

"Well, don't fret," Sheriff told him. "The same prankster that let your llamas out last week sneaked into the dog pound the same day and let out all the dogs." He took a big gulp of his tea. "Some folks just have a lousy sense of humor."

But Doc wasn't happy. We finished the meal in silence.

Chapter Eight
New Projects

Nobody was very happy on Friday night. Doc and Mrs. Ericson worried and fretted after the sheriff left; so the three of us went out to the bunkhouse. Scruggs didn't seem to have much to say. I think we were all thinking the same thing: we didn't believe in ghosts. But in the dark, with the wind coming up, it was still easy to be scared. Maybe not of ghosts, but of criminal camp owners who had never been brought to justice, of wandering pranksters who let penned animals loose, and of the lonely sound of the wind blowing off the dark lake.

Since Mom and Dad wouldn't be back with Jean until Sunday afternoon, we wouldn't be going home until then, either. Monday was Labor Day, and then school would start. At the moment, thoughts of school and Peabody, Wisconsin, seemed very homey and comfortable.

What was worse was that Jack and Scruggs went right to their room, leaving me to go to mine. At the moment, thoughts of Jean's coming were not unwelcome.

The dinner gong was going pretty hard the next morning—early. I got into my clothes and stumbled outside to get to breakfast.

Doc Ericson still looked pretty chagrined at the way the county commissioners had treated him, but he dug into his pancakes with a will. Jack and Scruggs were almost late for breakfast. Once everybody was seated and eating, Doc Ericson said, "Order for the morning is clearing debris from Pasture 2. Put the rocks you find in piles and burn the wood."

We all nodded. He added, "Kerosene's in the tool shed and there's a disposable lighter on the shelf. Better take some shovels, too. Make sure you light the fire away from trees."

It was just seven when we left to go to work, and we spent the next four hours in the field with our backs bent. Doc had about four kerosene cans of five gallons each in the tool shed, but we just took one.

Let me tell you, lugging a five-gallon can by a metal handle is no fun. The handle digs into your hand, the can swings around, and after about ten steps you think your arm's going to break. I staggered with it from the shed as far as the gate to Pasture 1, and then Jack took it.

Of course, all the llamas thought it was a bucket of food, so they crowded around us and kept trying to look at it and nibble at the cap.

Jack switched off to Scruggs and helped me shoo a path through the llamas to the gate of Pasture 2, which was open so the llamas could roam around. We switched off a few more times until we set it down at the far end of Pasture 2.

"Now this makes sense," Jack said, surveying the big patch of ground that was littered with broken boards,

New Projects

bits of roofing, nails, and rocks. "This part of the island is low-lying. The campers' cabins were here and got wrecked when the place flooded."

"There ought to be more wreckage than this," Scruggs said.

"Some's rotted away over the years, I guess," I said.

"And maybe kids have come out to pick up the bigger scraps," Jack added.

"Hmm. Well, come on then," Scruggs said, and we went to work.

The llamas, meanwhile, had given up on finding anything to eat in the kerosene can. We began piling up rocks in one place and wood in another. When we'd made a big enough pile of wood in a sandy spot, Jack doused it with kerosene. I had the lighter, and I waited until he took the can about twenty paces away before I lit the wood.

"All we need is some marshmallows," Scruggs said as the flames came up.

Doc Ericson came bouncing over the pasture in his jeep.

"Everything under control?" he called over the engine.

"Sure," Jack called back.

"I'm going to see Sheriff Duncan," he told us. "My wife'll be around to keep an eye on things. Careful with the fire, all right?"

We nodded and waved and went back to work. There's nothing remarkable about clearing land. But the llamas, though they lost interest in us, kept coming up to the fire. It seemed to fascinate some of them. I was a little worried about their woolly coats catching on fire—that's how close to the flames they were getting.

It made Scruggs nervous, too. He kept shooing them away. Finally we put everything aside and chased them all back into Pasture 1. Indignant and huffy, they galloped away from us, and we closed the gate after them.

The rest of the morning wore on. At last we heard the gong for lunch. Usually, afternoon chores were of the "fun" type, and that day was no disappointment. After lunch Doc Ericson took us to the barn. He pulled a confused tangle of straps and buckles off a hook on the wall.

"This is a saddle," he told us, "for a pony cart."

He had one of the gelding males, a brown and black llama named Beans, tethered on a short lead outside. "Beans has been broken to the saddle and harness," he told us. "But I haven't had a chance to get him hitched to the pony cart. And now I don't have time. So I thought I'd leave it to you."

We all looked from him to the so-called "saddle." I couldn't make sense out of it, but he got it over Beans's back and started adjusting lengths. Beans just glanced at him and flicked an ear.

It had a chest strap, like any harness, and there were two straps to fit around the llama's neck. Another long, thick strap went around the back of him, under his tail, and of course a cinch strap tightened under his barrel.

Once Doc Ericson got the body harness on him, it made more sense. He slipped a halter onto Beans, attached two reins, and ran them through a ring on the body harness.

"Now the thing with llamas," he told us, "is that you don't use a bit with them like you do on a horse.

New Projects

You've got to know that the llama will do what you want before you go out riding with him."

He took up the reins and stood behind the llama.

"Gee-yup," he said, and clicked with his tongue.

Beans trotted across the yard.

"Whoo-ooa," he said.

Beans stopped.

"Gee-yup."

Beans started again. Doc Ericson turned him to the right and brought him back to us. "Easy, huh?" he asked.

"Looks easy," Jack said.

"Now all you've got to do is get him hitched to the cart," Doc told us.

Chapter Nine
A Breathless Ride

Doc Ericson left us to ourselves for the rest of the afternoon. Getting Beans hitched to the pony cart was no real problem. He had to inspect the cart first, which he did by running his nose all along its frame and the rims of the wheels.

We walked him between the two hitching poles to get him used to them, and he didn't mind when we backed him up to the cart.

But when we hitched him to it, and he felt the weight behind him and the two restricting poles on either side, he put his ears back and swiveled his neck back to look at the poles. Then he looked at us as though to tell us he was ready to be turned loose.

Jack was standing by the cart holding the reins. I had clipped a lead onto Beans's halter. To start his training, we'd decided to keep one person in front and one on either side.

"Gee-yup," Jack said, and clicked his tongue.

I pulled on the lead.

Beans took one step, felt the cart following him, and bucked.

He bucked like crazy. He went up on his hind legs and tried to turn to the right to jump over the poles of the cart. Then he swung to the left to try it again. The lightweight, two-wheeled cart nearly tipped over. It went up on one wheel and then the other. But the low-slung pony cart—or sulky, as they are called—had a lot of spring to it. It bounced and jounced around, but it wasn't damaged.

Beans had flipped the lead rope right out of my hand. He jumped forward, and when the cart followed him, he reared up again.

Scruggs grabbed the lead rope with both hands, and I got a hold on the halter. Beans didn't like it and he spit, but Scruggs ducked and it just glanced off his shoulder.

"Easy, Beans," he said. "Easy does it." He worked his way up the lead so that Beans couldn't swing his head up. I had the halter, so Beans couldn't twist his head away, either.

"Try again, Jack," Scruggs said. "Penny, you stay on that side and I'll stay on this side. Don't let him get his head free."

We were all still for a second, and then Jack said, "Gee-yup!" and clicked his tongue.

Beans shuddered and stepped, struggled to get his head, took another step as we urged him along, then another, then another. We got him to pull the empty cart along until he would do it without Scruggs and me holding on. Then we unhitched the cart.

Jack had pretty well figured out the body harness. He got it off, and we took off the reins, but we left the halter on. A halter won't bother a llama or prevent him from eating and drinking freely, and it makes him

A Breathless Ride

easier to catch. We rewarded Beans with a capful of grain and put him in with the other llamas.

Jack wanted Scruggs and him to go back to their room, but Scruggs wanted to sit up on the fence and watch the llamas. I didn't say much, but I wanted them to sit on the fence, too. It seemed as though Jack was hung up on being friends with Scruggs and not letting anyone else in.

In the end we sat on the fence.

"School starts Tuesday," Scruggs said. He was a year ahead of me in school—ninth grade—but it was only his second year in Peabody Christian School. He'd never had some of the teachers he'd be getting.

We talked about some of the teachers. Jack was only going into seventh—just coming out of sixth—so he didn't have much to say. He looked annoyed. I felt like telling him to grow up, but I didn't say anything. The only way to keep Jack from edging me out was to get Scruggs to like talking to me. So I worked on that.

After about an hour's rest, we caught Beans again. It took a while to get his body harness on, but with all three of us working on it, we managed. We clipped the reins and the lead on and backed him between the poles of the cart.

He didn't seem to mind the weight this time, although he ran his nose up one of the poles to inspect it.

We got him fastened in, and then Scruggs and I took our places on either side of his head, and Jack stood by the cart, holding the reins as he had before.

"Gee-yup!" Jack said, and Llama Beans pranced like a pony around the barnyard.

Jack turned him a couple of times and at last said "Whoa!" and reined him in. Scruggs and I immediately gave him some grain and told him what a great llama he was.

"I think he's ready to drive," Jack said. "He's not scared of the cart anymore."

"No brakes on a cart," Scruggs observed. "If Beans takes off, you won't have much to stop him with."

"We've got to risk it sometime," Jack pointed out.

Scruggs gave a shrug, and I said, "Okay by me."

So Jack got in the cart. Scruggs and I stayed alongside Beans, each with a hand on the harness.

"Gee-yup!" And Jack clucked his tongue.

Beans started off, heedless of the added weight. He did so well that we let him go up the dirt road in front of the house and past the tool shed.

Jack turned him and got him up into a trot. Of course Scruggs and I dropped back.

Everything was going fine until Mrs. Ericson came walking out of the barn with a bucket of feed in her hand.

Beans turned his trot into a gallop.

"Hey, whoa!" Jack called, and pulled. The gallop became a frantic run as Beans clattered down the slope to the barnyard, anxious to get to Mrs. Ericson before she got through the gate.

"Jack, stop him!" I yelled.

The lightweight pony cart—dancing on its many springs—careened from side to side as it went speeding around the curve behind the llama. I could see that Jack was pulling back as hard as he could on the reins. I heard him yell something.

"What'd he say?" I asked Scruggs as we ran down towards the barnyard.

A Breathless Ride

"I think it was something like 'Yaaaggh!' " Scruggs said.

Mrs. Ericson had gone around the side of the far barn to measure the grain. We caught one glimpse of Beans flying after her and the pony cart skittering around the corner on one wheel with Jack still in the driver's seat.

"He's got magnets in his pants," Scruggs muttered and ran past me. "Anybody else would have gotten thrown out of that cart by now."

We heard the crash when the cart finally tipped over, and we raced around the corner of the barn.

Jack was on his feet—although the cart was on its side—and Beans had his muzzle deep in the bucket. Mrs. Ericson was letting him eat it. She looked a little shaken. I guess the sight of Beans and Jack tearing around the corner and bearing down on her scared her.

"Are you all right?" Scruggs asked, getting to Jack first.

"Yeah, somehow when I heard the cart crash I was already out and on my feet," Jack said. "I just found myself standing here holding the reins."

Scruggs let out a sigh of relief. We righted the cart. It didn't seem damaged. Pony carts as a rule are springy and lightweight. And, happily for Jack, llamas don't run as fast as horses.

We hooked a lead on Beans and unharnessed him from the cart.

Jack didn't say much, but he looked kind of white.

"Maybe we won't try this again until next weekend," he said.

Mrs. Ericson agreed.

Chapter Ten
Tragedy at Night

It had clouded up during our training sessions, and as we returned to the house to wash up for dinner, the breeze suddenly became quite cool.

Mrs. Ericson threw open the windows, and the wind fanned the hot kitchen.

"Storm tonight," Doc Ericson predicted. We sat down to beef stew and sourdough bread and milk. There were seconds all around, and Scruggs had thirds.

"Saw you tried the sulky," Doc Ericson said.

"Yeah, we tried," Jack admitted.

Doc Ericson was merrier that night than he had been. He grinned at Jack. "Takes more than an afternoon to make a pacer out of a llama, but you did all right."

Jack merely rolled his eyes.

"Honest," Doc said. "You got him hitched. You didn't spook him by yelling. You kept your seat and your head. Try again next Saturday. Just keep the discipline tight on Beans. He's got to know that the reins rule—even over food."

As he was talking, there was a bang of thunder that made everyone jump, and then a *woosh* of pouring rain.

"I'd better open up the barns," Doc said. Other than a brood stall in one barn and two stalls with restraining chutes in the other, the barns had no partitions on the ground floor so that the llamas could crowd into them for shelter. In summer llamas usually prefer the cool wetness outside to the inside of a barn, but Doc opened up the barns in bad weather.

Doc and Scruggs donned slickers and went out to get the doors open. Jack and I helped clear up from dinner.

The rain didn't let up all evening. Jack and Scruggs played checkers, and I sat in the rocking chair and twiddled my thumbs. The Ericsons had a lot of bookkeeping to do, and they worked at the kitchen table with their ledgers and adding machine.

About eight o'clock I gave up finding something to do, put on one of the slickers hanging in the coat room by the back door, and went to the bunkhouse.

My room in the bunkhouse had a bunk bed, a chest of drawers, and a narrow closet. The floor was plain concrete with braided rugs thrown on top.

I climbed onto the second bunk and picked up an old tattered copy of *Treasure Island* that I'd found in the big house.

I must have fallen asleep pretty quickly, I guess. I never did hear Jack and Scruggs slam the door of the farmhouse, nor did I hear them clatter onto the bunkhouse porch and go into their room.

But suddenly Jack was pounding on my door and yelling, "Alarm! Alarm! The lights are on! Let's go!"

"Here I come!" I yelled, and jumped off the bunk bed. I was still completely dressed, and I ran out,

Tragedy at Night

snatching the slicker as I went. The downpour of rain took my breath away as I raced into the sheets of water.

Scruggs, thrusting his head into a sweatshirt, was fumbling out the door of their room. The floodlights were on all over the front yard, the barns, and part of Pasture 1.

"Dogs!" Scruggs cried. We raced toward the barns. He scooped up a stout branch and thrust it into my hands. Jack and Dr. Ericson came racing toward us from the barns.

"Guns!" they screamed. "Get the guns!" We all turned and ran into the house in a jumble. We followed Dr. Ericson to his study in the back where the gun cabinet was.

"A whole pack of dogs," he cried. "They're attacking the herd. Scruggs, you take the one rifle, I'll—" He pulled on the door of the glass cabinet. "Where's the key?" he yelled. "Who took the key?" He swept his hand across the top of the cabinet. "Who took the key?"

"Get back!" Scruggs exclaimed. He picked up a chair and smashed the front of the cabinet with it. The glass shattered and fell all over the floor. Doc and Scruggs took the rifles, and we ran out again.

"Stay back!" Doc cried as we got to the barnyard. He and Scruggs fired at shadows on the edge of the darkness. The rain was pouring so hard that I hadn't noticed the snarls of the dogs, but suddenly they turned to yelps of pain.

In the dimly lit margin of the lighted area, I saw one of the six-month crias crumpled on the ground. Its mother had a dog at her own neck, but all it had gotten hold of was llama wool. Scruggs's rifle barked again, and the freed llama leaped clear, but she stayed by her fallen baby.

Doc and Jack rushed into the darkness. The llamas, at sight of us, rushed for the safety of the barnyard. I heard Doc's rifle fire several more times.

The cria on the ground was bleeding. I still had the slicker in my hand. I threw it over the injured baby llama. It opened its eyes and struggled, and I managed to pick it up.

"Get it to the house!" Scruggs called.

I ran for the house and met Mrs. Ericson. She had a pair of high-powered lights. I took the lights and gave her the baby.

I guess everyone has a night that he calls the worst night of his life, and this night was my worst. I got a light to Jack. We would sweep the pastures with the lights for Scruggs and Doc, and they would shoot at any dogs they saw. Meanwhile, Mrs. Ericson was at work on the injured crias and adults. She had Doc's Colt .45 handgun to protect the barnyard, but no more dogs ventured under the floodlights.

Doc sent Scruggs back to help in first aid, but he and Jack and I had to cover the whole pasturage with the searchlights and rifle. We found two crias in Pasture 2. They were dead. The dogs had dragged them there. I thought Doc would fly into a rage, but he surprised me. He put his arm across my shoulders and asked, "Can you stand this? Are you all right?"

"Yes," I told him. "I'm okay. Let's go."

So we all plodded on in the driving rain. The hogwire on the fence was unbroken as far as we could see. But Pasture 4 had a gate that opened out to a dirt service road, and that gate was wide open when we got to it.

"This is where they got in," Doc called, and he closed the gate.

We picked our way around the debris in Pasture 4 and went into Pasture 2, closing that gate also. Then we entered Pasture 1 and at last the barnyard.

Scruggs was there alone.

"There's a female dead," he told Doc, "and two in the brood stall that need you. Two crias are up at the house."

"Okay. You stand guard. Jack, you'll assist me here. Penny, you help my wife at the house. And if you get a chance, put coffee on. It's going to be a long night."

Chapter Eleven
Jean Comes Home

I didn't notice when the rain stopped, nor when the sun rose, a watery yellow and gray light in the morning. We had the two injured crias bundled into sleeping bags in the front room. They were stitched up where they'd been bitten and torn, but the shock and exposure had hurt them, too. We'd bottle-fed them during the night with warm formula.

The crias were in a kind of stupor and would moan sometimes. One of them could be returned to its mother, but the other was an orphan now. The Ericsons would have to hand-raise it.

I'd dozed off and on during the night, but about 7:00 A.M., I fell asleep on the rug between the two crias.

Doc had promised Dad to get us to church, but he never even came up from the barn until after ten, and when he did, it was with Sheriff Duncan. They were going out to collect the dogs that had been shot.

Mrs. Ericson and I bottle-fed the babies again. Of course I'd been drenched with rain when I'd come in the night before; so that morning I had on a collection of clothes that she'd found for me.

Llamas on the Loose

About noon Jack and Scruggs came dragging up from the barn. They'd helped to collect the dogs—not a pleasant job.

"Pound dogs," was all Scruggs said.

"That's what I figured," Mrs. Ericson said. "Once they'd been let loose from the dog pound, they formed a pack and went hunting." Doc had told us that strays and even licensed dogs will go after llamas, just like dogs will go after rabbits. We'd heard stories about llama farmers who had lost animals to packs of neighborhood dogs.

"But who opened the gate to Pasture 4 for them?" Jack asked.

"That gate's got a bad latch on it," Mrs. Ericson said. "A dog that's been farm-raised might get it open. Or even the men that were up there on the service road putting in a drainage pipe this week might have shut it without checking the latch." She stood up. "Come have breakfast."

"I'll help," I said. I could see she was tired.

"We'll all help," Jack added.

She glanced at us and gave a half-smile. "Fine."

Even though we all pitched in to help with breakfast, it was a silent and dreary meal. Doc had been up all night and all morning. He sat glumly shoveling eggs into his mouth, chewing and swallowing like a machine.

Finally Mrs. Ericson said, "What'd Sheriff say? Anything?"

Instead of answering the question, he said, "Who are we kidding? The whole town's against us. Everybody."

We all looked up at him.

"First, they hid the truth about this place. Now they're hounding us with old zoning laws. People are letting our livestock loose or setting dogs on us," he said. "Another night like last night will ruin us."

"Might be a run of bad luck," she said.

"This can't be just bad luck," he told her. "Why'd they bring us in if all they wanted to do was drive us out again?"

Mrs. Ericson was silent for a moment, and then she said, "We can't pull up stakes now."

He looked at her. "I know. We've got to stand and fight."

"Us too," Scruggs said. "Whatever's going on, we're on your side. Maybe we can help."

Doc suddenly smiled a sad but gentle smile. "You kids did better than most adults would have done last night."

"I think the Lord must have helped us," Scruggs said. "Because we were pretty scared—at least I was."

"Me, too," Jack said, and I agreed.

Doc looked us over and smiled again, a little ruefully. "Well, whoever helped you—thank you. We'll all fight it out together. Starting next week, you'll be sitting watch at nights. I guess the fun's over."

"And Jean'll be here," Scruggs added. "She can help, too. She's a smart kid." Jack and I glanced at each other but didn't say anything.

Although Doc looked bone weary, he drove us home. We were mostly silent throughout the long, two-hour trip, except for once when Jack said, "I wonder where the cabinet key was."

"Let's just be glad that the glass wasn't shatter proof," Doc said, "or we'd have lost a lot more llamas before we got those rifles out."

For myself, I was really thankful that Ticktock—my favorite—and Beans were unharmed. I liked Beans a lot, too, but he was also really valuable because of the training he'd had.

As I sat with my head back on the top of the back seat, I recalled my dad's observation that whoever had let the llamas out had gotten us all out of the house. And Jack had told him that nothing had been stolen.

What about the key to the gun cabinet?

Somebody had turned loose all the dogs from the dog pound the same day that the llamas were let out. Had someone guessed that the dogs would find the farm? It was likely that they would: the lake was shallow between the island and the near shore. If the dogs had gotten wind of the llamas, they could have easily splashed across and come up through the trees.

Or had someone brought them? Brought them and opened the gate for them? We might never find a clue. There were men working on the farm on weekdays, and the whole island was trampled up with footprints and tire tracks.

Doc didn't stop in when he brought us home.

"Tell your Dad I'll give him a call," he said, and then he pulled out to take Scruggs home.

My little sister Jean was glad to see us when we came in. Mom and Dad had told her all about the llama farm on the way up, and I guess she had a lot to tell us. But as soon as we walked in, Mom said, "What's happened? You two look like you've seen combat!"

So we told her and Dad—and Jean, of course—about all that had happened. Jean listened, cocked an eyebrow, and went to finish her unpacking.

Jean Comes Home

Jack and I looked at each other, but just then Dad said, "It's a hard blow on them, all right. But it might be hasty to suppose that the town's trying to drive them out. Troubles come, and sometimes they come all at once."

Jack and he and Mom sat and talked about it, but I went upstairs to see Jean.

"Hi," she said when I walked in. Jean had been having loads of adventures down in Alabama. She'd brought back all kinds of souvenirs and some photos, too. We talked about them for a while, but she didn't once mention the llama farm. So finally I said, "Think you might come up to the llama farm next weekend?"

She shrugged. "I don't know. I don't think I could stand all the troubles up there."

"Like what?"

"Like llamas getting attacked by dogs. And guns and all."

"It's not so bad." I suddenly wondered what I would do if Jean didn't come. Jack was having lots of fun with Scruggs, and I didn't like being the odd man out.

"It sounds bad," she said.

"Where's your spirit of adventure?"

"I have no spirit of adventure." She glanced over at me. "None. It's true."

"What about everything you did in Alabama?" I asked her. "Explored a cave, found a deserted hunting lodge? Wasn't that an adventure?"

Jean looked at me. "I learned something new," she said. "And it's this: I was trying to prove something to everybody. Well, now I see I didn't have to prove anything to anybody. Uncle Rufus helped me see it all: God doesn't love me because I'm brave; so I don't have to try to be brave. He doesn't even love me because I'm good, because I'm *not* good. I was a real rat while I was in Alabama. The only way God can love me is because Jesus died for me."

I shrugged. "Okay. I believe that."

"That means I don't have to tag along after you and Jack," she said. "I was trying to prove something. But now I know for myself."

"What?" I asked.

"I guess I know that I'm me. God made me this way, and He made you your way."

I just blinked at her. At last I heard myself say, "You've really changed."

She just looked at me, and so I said, "Okay, forget the adventure part. What about the llamas? They're really funny, and they're smart, too, and gentle."

"I don't know." She went back to putting her stuff away.

I didn't know what else to say until I remembered a new point. "Scruggs wants you to come."

"Sure," she said.

"It's true. Ask Mom. Scruggs suggested for you to come," I told her. "He told Jack and me that he feels bad about how he used to pick on you so much."

She stopped again and looked at me. "Are you serious?"

"Yes. Like it or not, Scruggs is all set to be friends with you."

She didn't know what to say. Jean likes to please people, so I knew I had her on the line. I just had to bring her in.

"He keeps reminding the Ericsons about you," I told her. "And you can ask Jack about that, or just ask

Scruggs. He'll tell you to your face that he wants you to come."

"Well, it does sound like llamas are fun," she admitted.

The thing to do now was just wait. Scruggs would back me up, and I knew Mom and Dad would want to get Jean involved on the farm with Jack and me. As for Jack, well, he was just going to have to get used to the idea of having Jean around. He wouldn't like it, but that's the way it was going to be.

Chapter Twelve
Night Watch

School started on Tuesday, and by Wednesday Jean was convinced. We walked to school every morning with Scruggs, and he was careful to be nice to Jean. I think it kind of hurt Jack's feelings to see Scruggs take so much time to talk with Jean or me or both of us. It finally dawned on me that even Scruggs was looking at us as a set. We all belonged together in his mind; so he was trying to be friends with all of us.

Well, on Friday Doc picked us up.

"What's the news?" Jack asked as we climbed into the car.

"Been a long week," he said wearily. "Is this Jean?" he asked.

She said yes and hello, and he told her he was glad to have her. Then he added, "I've been up all night every night this week. You four are going to have to take a turn at keeping watch."

"Did Sheriff find out who let those dogs loose from the dog pound?" Scruggs asked.

"No. The trail is cold, I'm afraid."

Llamas on the Loose

At first I was afraid that Doc would let only Jack and Scruggs stand watch at night, but it wasn't so. Jean and I stayed at the barn from dark until eleven that night, and then Jack took it from 11:00 P.M. to 3:00 A.M., and Scruggs had it from 3:00 A.M. until dawn.

Once dark came, we drove the llamas into the two barns and the barnyard, and we closed the gate to Pasture 1. They didn't really like being crowded together under the glare of the floodlights, but llamas are very adaptable.

There was a rifle kept in the barn, now, hung up in the feed room. It would be out of sight from visitors, but very handy to one of us if we had to use it.

I had read in Amy Belle mystery stories about how Amy Belle and her buddies Muffy and Flip had to stand watch. Somehow those stories never got it across to me how absolutely dull and boring it can be to stay in one place for four hours. Or how long four hours can be. When Amy Belle stood watch, something always happened.

We were in plain sight of the farmhouse, and Doc had hung up a metal triangle in one of the barns for us to ring if trouble came. So it wasn't like we were all alone. We weren't scared—just bored and sleepy.

The llamas settled down after a while. They can lie like cats do, with their legs tucked under them and their heads up. When long-necked llamas are lying like that, it looks like a field of periscopes.

Jean liked the llamas well enough. I'd introduced her personally to Ticktock.

"Kind of dirty, isn't she?" Jean asked. "Looks like she's been rolling in ashes."

Night Watch

"Ticktock!" I said. The llama looked at me and checked my jacket pocket for grain. "Were you rolling in our ashes?"

Llamas do like to roll in dust, dirt, and sand. I guess we could add ashes to the list.

"Maybe that's why they wanted to hang around the fire," I said to Jean. I told her about how the llamas were so attracted to the flames.

"These are the weirdest animals I've ever seen," she said.

I shrugged. "God made them."

"He made the duckbilled platypus, too," she added. "I guess He thought some animals ought to make us laugh."

"Doc says llamas evolved," I told her.

"What do you say when he tells you that?" she asked.

"The truth. That God created llamas."

She nodded. "What does he say to that?"

"Oh, he tells me that when I've been to school as long as he has, then I'll understand these things more."

She shook her head. "Dad's been to school as much as Doc has, and he believes God created llamas."

We stationed ourselves on the edge of the wagon that Doc hauled hay in. We dangled our legs over the side and looked out over the herd. The injured llama was back with the herd, and so were the two crias. The orphan was in pretty good shape, but the other was blind in one eye, and its left ear was ruined—it no longer stood up and part of it was gone. The stitches still showed.

I watched the cria as it lay sphinxlike alongside its mother, with its blind side to her and its other eye watching the rest of the world. That little llama had been perfect, especially in its legs. Llamas are often a bit knock-kneed, but this one had been perfect. It could have been a champion. But now . . .

"It can be the father of a champion," Jean said when I told her how sad it was for that one to be ruined. "If it's got what it takes to be a perfect llama, it can father a perfect llama—as long as it has a good mate."

"I guess so."

Nothing happened that night. Jack relieved us at 11:00 P.M., and we went to bed.

The next morning Doc let us sleep later than usual, but otherwise the order for the day was the same: clearing rocks and debris.

We took turns lugging the kerosene can to Pasture 2.

"This is ridiculous," Jean gasped. "There are so many cans of kerosene in the barn—couldn't we store this one in the field somewhere?"

"Don't be silly," Jack said.

"I think it's a good idea," Scruggs told her. "The cans are waterproof. It shouldn't hurt them any to leave them out overnight."

Jack looked a little miffed, but he didn't protest any more. Scruggs found a hollow in the ground that was covered with tall grass. We arranged the grass as well as we could to shed rain, and then we went to work.

In the afternoon we hitched Beans to the sulky. It had been a while since he'd seen it, but he seemed to remember all that we'd taught him.

This time I got in the sulky so Scruggs and Jack could pull back on Beans's harness to stop him on command. We stationed Jean back by the barn with a bucket of feed.

Night Watch

We opened the barnyard gate and brought Beans up the hill. He obeyed the commands and turned perfectly.

"Okay," Jack said. "We'll stay right on his harness. When Jean comes out, say 'Whoa,' and we'll pull back to make him stop."

"Got it," I told him.

We started Beans, and Jean stepped out from the barn with the feed bucket.

"Whoa," I said. Jack and Scruggs pulled back on the halter. Beans flirted his head and broke their grasp.

"Whoa!" I yelled, and hauled back.

"Penny, stop!" Jack yelled as we thundered past. Jean saw us hurtling down towards her. Instead of standing still and holding the bucket out, she ran into the barn.

"No, Jean!" I called.

Beans ran after her. The sulky was swinging back and forth, bouncing on all its springs. One wheel hit the open barn door. Beans suddenly slid to a stop as he got Jean cornered with the bucket.

I guess I flew out of the sulky onto the ground just outside the barn door. I kind of heard myself land (with a thump) and felt a pain between my shoulder blades. Next thing I knew, Jack and Scruggs were pulling me to my feet.

"This was a bad idea," I said.

"No kidding," Jack told me.

"You okay, Jean?" Scruggs asked, stepping around Beans, who had his nose buried in the bucket.

"Sure, fine," she said. "It just scared me a little when he ran after me."

I rolled my eyes to Jack. "*She* was scared."

Chapter Thirteen
Back to Normal

The weather really cooled off, and by the next Saturday morning we were glad to build up a fire when we worked in the pastures. We had the kerosene cans dotted around Pastures 2 and 4, hidden under makeshift shelters of old planks, branches, and grass. The arrangement was that each Saturday one of us would grab the lighter, and that person was in charge of setting the fires and watching to make sure that they didn't get out of control.

Pasture 4—the part that was unworked—was a mess. It was dotted with trees up in one corner, and the ground was uneven. Jack took a tumble when he didn't watch where he was going. We heard him yell just as he toppled down into a wide ditch in the ground.

"You all right?" Scruggs called as we ran up to him.

"Ouch, yes," he said, and sat up. "What's this hole doing here?" He looked around. We were standing at the edge of it. Wild field grass had grown inside it and filled it up, and the sides of it were worn down and eroded.

"It does look like somebody dug it out once," I said.

"Maybe one of the cabins was here," Scruggs guessed. "Or a laundry room or something. Something with some type of foundation dug into the ground."

Jack stood up, and Scruggs gave him a hand out of the hole.

"Hey, where's Jean?" Jack asked.

Just then, as though in answer, we heard her call, "Over here!"

We turned and saw her by the trees, right where the fence wound its way into them. She was standing on uneven ground. She waved and yelled, "There's another one over here!"

"Big deal," Jack mumbled under his breath, but Scruggs's interest perked. "Let's go see," he said, and Jack and I followed.

Jean had found another of the old dug-out foundations. It had chunks of old concrete still embedded in the corners.

"I guess the flood broke up the foundations," Jack said.

"And probably whatever wreckers the county sent out finished the job," Scruggs added.

"We could have a good time out here playing flashlight tag," Jack said.

"Gotta be dark to play flashlight tag," Scruggs reminded him.

"Doc might let us," Jack said. "Now that things are calming down."

Just then we heard the dinner gong ring.

"Uh-oh," Jack said. We took off for the farmhouse.

"Don't look so scared," Doc called. "I just wanted to know if anyone felt like going to town with me."

Back to Normal

Jean came panting up last of all. Scruggs held out his hand to have her come up and join us. "How about going to town?" he asked her.

"Jean and Penny have to help get lunch," Jack said, and this time his annoyance was plain.

"Since when?" I demanded. "We've all helped with lunch before."

Doc backed me up. "Share and share alike," he said. "The good times and the bad. Any or all of you can come."

So we all climbed into the jeep with him. He had the canvas sides up to protect us from the chill air. Jack and I were silent on the way to town. He and I and Scruggs were squeezed into the back, with Jean up front. She and Scruggs and Doc talked about the flood and the old foundations we had found.

Jack at last got over his grumpiness enough to ask if we could go out and play flashlight tag in Pasture 4 some evening.

"Well, I don't mind," Doc said. "But somebody's got to watch the llamas, and I'm afraid you'll have to get a flashlight. I don't want to waste the batteries of the farm searchlights."

So then Jack and I got out our money to see if we could buy one. He'd spent his one paycheck so far on a canteen with a cloth cover and a belt to hang it on. I'd forgotten to bring my purse with me that weekend, though I had some change in my pocket.

Scruggs always uses his money to purchase stuff for his experiments or to put away for college. All he had was a dollar. Jean hadn't been paid yet, of course. But she did offer fifty cents. Doc dropped us off at Ernie's Everything Outlet.

"I have to go see Sheriff Duncan," he told us. "I'll take you back as soon as I get finished."

He parked, and we all got out.

All put together, we had two dollars and sixty-three cents.

"That ought to get a decent flashlight," Scruggs said. "Let's go see."

Ernie's Everything Outlet did have flashlights for sale. We found one in our price range. Then Jack remembered that we had to get batteries, too.

"Rats," he said. "We'll never make it."

"Well, by next week we'll all have our pay," Scruggs said. "We can do it next Saturday night."

Nothing seemed to be going Jack's way that morning, but all he said was, "I guess you're right."

We bought soft drinks instead and went out in front of Ernie's to wait for Doc.

"Say," I said as Jack and Scruggs leaned against the jeep.

"What?" Scruggs asked. They all followed my gaze. I had spotted the young, dark-haired guy with the sunglasses who had come to the farm about the zoning problems.

"That's the guy who wanted to survey the place," I said. "Sheriff's been trying to get a hold of him."

He was coming out of a Laundromat up the street, carrying a clothes basket stuffed full with clean laundry.

"I'll go talk to him," I said. "Doc and Sheriff'll both be glad we found him." I went up after the guy and called out to him.

I got him just as he was trying to get into his car.

Back to Normal

"Excuse me," I said while he balanced the clothes basket on one knee against the car and fished for his keys.

He took one look at me, thrust the whole basket of clothes at me, unlocked the door while I juggled the basket, and ducked into his car.

"Hey!" I called.

He pulled out with a roar and shot away.

"Stop!" I called. "I've got your clothes!"

Jean came running up. Without thinking, I shoved the clothes basket at her and went running down the sidewalk after the car. Jack followed me. "Where are we running?" he asked me.

"After that yellow VW!" I shouted. "Get the license plate number!"

But the car was way ahead of us at Winneca's one and only stoplight, which was—at that moment—green. The car went around the corner and was gone.

I stopped in my tracks; so did Jack.

"You get it?" I asked.

"Nothing," he said. "What'd the guy do, run away from you?"

"And how!" I told him. "He didn't even take his laundry." I glanced back at Jean and Scruggs, who were bent over the basket, looking through it.

"Here we go again," Jack said. "More mystery."

"It was a different car," I told him. "When he showed up at the farm, he had a four-door, midnight blue Ford. Nice. Now he's in an old, dirty, yellow VW."

"Like he was faking us out," Jack said.

"Yeah," I told him. "Like he was faking us out. I wonder why."

Chapter Fourteen
The New Team

"That sheriff's going to want these clothes," Jean said when Jack and I walked up to them. "Start looking."

I felt annoyed. "For what?"

"Name tags, hotel towels, anything," she said. "Maybe we can track him down."

"She's right," Scruggs said. "Hurry up."

So we stooped over the basket with them.

We rummaged through a lot of socks and underwear, then came to layers of faded jeans and ratty T-shirts and sweatshirts.

"Nothing," Scruggs said. "Nothing you wouldn't find in anybody's clothes basket."

"He doesn't have name tags, anyway," Jean observed.

"Whoever heard of putting name tags on jeans and old shirts?" Jack asked. "This idea was no good. We should have fanned out to track him."

"Well, at least we know he lives in a place where there's no laundry machine," Jean said.

Jack snorted. "Big deal."

"Cool it, Jack," Scruggs told him. They looked at each other over the clothes basket.

Jean didn't pay any attention to them. "But he must be poor. I mean, these clothes are just about in rags."

"Hey," I said. "No shirts—no men's shirts." Scruggs glanced at me. "You know," I said, "shirts with collars. When I saw that guy, he was wearing a suit, like he was just now. And he was driving a nice car, dark blue. Like he was a businessman or somebody official, you know—"

"White collar," Scruggs said. "That's what you mean."

"Yeah, a white-collar worker."

He looked at the clothing. "Well, if clothes make the man, these clothes make our man a fake."

Just then Doc came out from the sheriff's office. We ran to tell him what had happened. He had us take the clothes basket to the sheriff.

Sheriff Duncan was surprised at our story. He asked some questions, but at last he said, "Well, it's a puzzle. But I can't say that the fellow's broken the law. I mean, did he ever *tell* anyone that he was working for the county?"

"No," Doc said. "When he came to the farm all dressed up, he introduced himself as representing the concerns of the county commissioners."

"Anybody can do that," Sheriff said. Sheriff Duncan was tall and thin and rugged-looking. He swung one leg up and perched on the edge of his desk. "And anybody can leave his laundry behind and run away if he wants. I don't think we have a criminal offense here."

"No, but we do have a suspicious character," Doc said. "One who might know something about who opened our gates and let the llamas loose."

"And who let the dogs out of the pound," I added.

The New Team

"Seems like we'd chalked that up to teen-age pranksters," Sheriff said. "But if it makes you feel better, I'll look into it."

We piled back into the jeep. Jack was in a bad mood. He sat in the front and talked with Doc. When we got back to the farm, I talked to him alone out by the bunkhouse.

"What's the matter with you?" I asked.

"What do you mean what's the matter with me?" he demanded. "Now all of a sudden you're on Jean's side, too."

"You didn't have to talk that way to her. She was right to look for a clue in the clothes basket. It was all we had."

"I thought you and me were partners," he said. "You sure don't act like one!"

"You're the one who tried to keep Scruggs all to yourself," I said. "Where was our partnership then? You never wanted me on the fences with you."

"Girls like you always get jealous."

"Oh, grow up, Jack!" And I turned to go to my room.

Jack went up toward the house. I passed Scruggs on the bunkhouse porch.

"What's wrong?" he asked.

"Nothing—except that Jack's acting like a baby," I said. "All because things aren't going his way."

"Maybe I'll get a chance to see what's bugging him," he said.

I looked at Scruggs. "I know what's bugging him."

He'd stepped off the porch, but he stopped and looked up at me. "He doesn't want Jean tagging along," I said.

"Oh. Hmm."

And Scruggs would have walked away, but I said, "Scruggs." He looked at me again.

"Why are you being so nice to her? Not just nice, extra nice," I said.

He put a foot up on the worn planks. "Don't you remember when we were little kids?" he said.

"When you lived on our street?" I asked.

"Yeah, I had a foster family on that street before I got moved down to Racine for a year," he said. "The Browns."

"Yeah?" I asked.

"Don't you remember anything else?"

"You drew chalk pictures on the sidewalk," I said.

"With my sister," he added.

"Was she your foster sister or your real sister?"

"She was my real sister." He lifted his head and looked right up at me. We were both silent. For the first time I saw Scruggs as somebody else—not as the rough, tough kid who'd gotten saved. Not as an older kid who I could be friends with. Not even as the Scruggs I knew at that moment: the experimenter, the builder. I saw him as I guess he was a long time ago—lonely and afraid and too young to understand why he was moved around. The Scruggs who had been too afraid to go out and meet the kids with "normal" families had spent his time drawing pictures on the sidewalk with his little sister.

"Where is she now?" I asked.

He just looked at me, and instead of really answering, he said, "I could never handle it. Even after I got saved, I never said much about her to Mother. But now she

The New Team

talks about it to me, sometimes. Still, I try never to think about it. I just can't."

"Is she just gone?" I asked. "Or is she—" But I stopped, because the word *dead* suddenly sounded too hard, too cruel. "Is she—" I faltered. "Did she—pass away?"

"Jean!" he yelled up to the bunkhouse. "It's time for lunch! Are you coming?"

"Okay!" She came running out and let the door bang behind her. "Sorry."

"That's okay. Let's go."

"I'll be up in a minute," I told them.

I went back into my room and wrote a note to Jack— *'The barn after lunch.'* Then I went up to the house for our late lunch.

After lunch and chores I went down to the barn and waited. A few minutes later Jack came down.

"What did you want?" he asked.

"To tell you something that Scruggs told me," I said.

"What's that?"

"Well, first, I'm sorry I told you to grow up."

"Oh, I don't care about that. What did you want to tell me?" he asked. I could see he was still mad.

"Scruggs talked to me."

"About what?"

"About Jean."

"Yeah?" He looked curious.

"I still want to be partners with you," I told him. "We always have been, and I hope we always will be."

He nodded and looked more sober. "Me, too," he said. "I want to be partners, but I want to be good friends with Scruggs, too."

"That's just it," I told him. "We'll always be partners, Jack, but right now we're part of a team. And Jean's a part of that team, too."

He looked down.

"Dad was right," I told him. "It's time to give Jean a break. And Scruggs is going to give her a break whether you like it or not."

"What did he say?" Jack asked.

"He told me about his little sister. I think—I think she died. A long time ago."

"He's never said anything to me about that!" Jack exclaimed.

"He likes Jean," I told him. "And that's why. I guess he and his little sister were close—like maybe he felt like he was taking care of her when they got moved around. Jean must remind him of her."

"But what happened?" Jack asked. "To his sister, I mean?"

I shrugged. "He didn't say. But he told me enough to let me know once and for all: he's on Jean's side."

"Man!" Jack leaned his head against the gate. "Why does everything bad happen to Scruggs?"

"You know what Dad says—it's a world of sorrows and sin."

"Yeah, but his parents *and* his sister."

"I'm not sure about his parents," I told Jack. "I think they're alive, but they gave up their kids. His dad's been in prison, I think."

Jack looked at me. "Why does God let people like that have kids? Doesn't He know what the kids go through?"

"Well, He saved Scruggs," I pointed out. "And He gave him a happy home, now."

The New Team

"That's true."

"And maybe He's given Jean to Scruggs so he can look out for her," I added.

"To make up for Scruggs's losing his sister."

Jack looked up at the big house. Scruggs and Jean were coming down to take out the sulky.

"Maybe you're right," he said. "Boy, Penny, I feel like a big baby, now. Jean's not so bad."

I didn't say anything to that, but I was glad he was sorry for the way he'd acted, and I didn't feel too proud of myself either.

"So now we're all a team," I told him. "Me and you and Scruggs and Jean."

"Okay." He nodded. As Jean and Scruggs came up, he swung the barnyard gate open for them.

"Sulky crash course time," Scruggs said with a grin.

"I'll get the feed bucket," Jean volunteered. She went off to Barn 2.

"I'm going to try to bring Beans in," Scruggs told us. "I got him haltered last time."

"Okay," Jack said. "Penny and I'll get the sulky."

He and I went into Barn 1.

"You're still my partner," he told me, and held out his hand. We shook on it. "And we'll be part of the team, too."

We took the sulky up by the poles and brought it out into the barnyard. Jean had the bucket, but Jack took it from her. "You can hold the lead on Beans if you want," he told her. "I already had my turn on it. Maybe next week you can drive, if he's calm enough."

"Thanks," Jean said. She went to get a lead.

Jack shot me a glance and smiled.

Chapter Fifteen
Tracking Down Clues

Scruggs found Beans lying in one of our old ash piles and haltered him with no difficulty. I think Beans had some kind of internal clock to tell him when it was Saturday afternoon and sulky time. And so far—since he'd gotten a bucket of grain every time we worked together—sulky time had been pretty pleasant. So he didn't object to being haltered and led into the barnyard.

We practiced riding him around, and he did well as long as there was no food in sight. But as soon as Jack showed up with the bucket, Beans lost all discipline and raced to get to it first. Jean and I tried to hold him back. Since we were prepared, we had better success, but Beans got rougher.

He finally broke away. Scruggs got dumped out of the cart. Sulkies are light and close to the ground, so if you get dumped out, you haven't got far to fall, as long as you fall out backwards or over the side. If the animal pulling the sulky were to stop suddenly, you'd get pitched forward into the harness and maybe get tangled up or driven over. But it didn't look like we were going to have any problems with Beans stopping suddenly. If we could get him to stop at all, we would have called it square and settled for that.

Jean and I helped Scruggs up, and we all went down to join Jack.

"The problem," Jean said, "is that Beans doesn't respect us. He knows we can't force him to obey."

Jack took the bucket back where Beans couldn't get it. The dinner gong rang.

"Time to go home," he said. "But I'm determined to think of something."

"Jean's right. We just have to make him respect our commands," Scruggs said.

Jack glanced from Scruggs to Jean, and I saw the old resentment pass quickly over his face, but he must have gotten it out of his head pretty quickly, because he nodded. "That's the problem. But I'll think of something." He slipped the halter off Beans and let him go back into Pasture 1.

Everybody felt cheerful in the car, but tired. It had been a busy day and a half.

"Maybe if Sheriff Duncan can track down that fella in the VW, we'll get somewhere," Doc said as the car trundled over the bridge that spanned the marshes and connected Winneca to the highway. "Say, look at that mud down there," he said. "All washed into the marshes. The drainage still isn't that good down here."

Jean suddenly sat up. She looked out the window. I was about to say something when Scruggs spoke up.

"Dr. Ericson, do you think someone's been doing all this stuff to the farm for a reason? Like revenge or jealousy or something?"

"I don't know what to think," Doc told him. "Sometimes I think it's just a string of misfortunes. Other times I think it must be an organized attempt to destroy the farm. But why would anyone want to destroy the farm? A crime has to have a motive behind it. What could the motive be?"

Scruggs of course didn't know, and Jack said, "Well, nothing's happened in a while. Maybe it was all coincidence."

"We'll have to wait and see," Doc told him. "But by all means we'll keep on our toes while we wait."

After that we talked about more cheerful things, and it wasn't until after we got home that Jean said anything about what she'd been thinking.

We were up in our room, pulling out our dirty clothes, when she turned around and said, "Did you see all that mud washed down into the marsh?"

"Yeah," I said. "Why?"

"Don't you remember the VW?"

I suddenly straightened up. The VW had been caked with mud, too. As though it had been driving through it, slogging around the edges of the marshland.

We looked at each other.

"Has Doc got a rowboat?" she asked.

"Sure, but we'll never have time to take it out."

"Unless we got up really early," she said.

I groaned. "Staying up on watch, hauling rocks around, and getting tossed out of a sulky aren't enough? Now we're going to get up some morning at the crack of dawn to row around the lake?"

"We might spot the VW," she said.

"You and your great ideas," I moaned. "But I do think you're right."

"Let's call a meeting and tell Jack and Scruggs," she said.

"Okay."

We told Jack about it, but we didn't get a chance to talk to Scruggs until Monday on the way to school. He approved of the idea of rowing along the shore and the marshes to find the yellow VW.

"Although," he added, "Doc might think it's crazy."

"We don't have to tell him what we're looking for," I pointed out. "That way he can't laugh at us."

"And that way if we do spot the car, we can surprise Doc with the news," Jack said. "Just like Amy Belle did in *The Secret of the Old High Heels.*"

"Did you read that one?" Jean asked.

He shrugged. "I glanced at it."

"Did you like it?" she asked.

"Well, you know—I guess I did like the part where Amy Belle used her pillowcases to signal the rescue pilot and bring him in for a safe landing over a mine field," he admitted.

"Yeah, I wish we could learn semaphore at our school like she did at hers," Jean said.

"Maybe in high school."

"Meanwhile," Scruggs said, "we take the boat out Saturday morning and keep an eye peeled."

"Right!" we all said.

"And if we spot the VW?" he asked.

"Close in on 'em!" Jack cried.

"Wrong!" Scruggs said. "We play it safe and head for town or the farm—whichever is closest."

That week, the cool weather continued. At night we had frost, but the sun by day would melt any ice that formed in the puddles and ruts of the road.

Friday afternoon we were ready when Doc got us.

"What's new?" Jack asked.

Tracking Down Clues

"One cria," he told us. "Born Thursday. How about you four? Anything new?"

Nothing much was new except that we had our flashlight for flashlight tag. We asked if we could go rowing on the lake, and Doc said we could. "As long as you wear life jackets," he told us. "We've got some that we found stored in the farmhouse."

"We can all swim," Jack told him.

"Not in winter water," he said. "Life jackets for all." We all agreed, and the talk shifted to the new cria that had been born.

"We named her Dolly Llama," Doc said. "She's a gem: all cream-colored with a brown tail. Maybe our luck is changing at last."

"Or God is answering our prayers," Scruggs added.

Doc glanced at him in the rearview mirror.

"That's true, too. I have to admit, it sure was a good idea to hire farmhands who pray. You guys cover all your bases."

"Do, uh, do you believe in God, Doc?" Scruggs asked.

"Sure, but I make it a point never to talk about religion," Doc said. "I might watch for it, but I never talk about it."

"I used to think that way, too," Scruggs said. "Except I never even used to watch for it. I used to think it was for the birds—believing in God and Jesus and all that."

"Of course, everyone's entitled to his opinion—" Doc began, but Scruggs went on. Jack looked a little embarrassed, but Jean watched Scruggs with interest.

"So you know what happened to me?" Scruggs asked. "This little old lady from the church in Peabody started being really nice to me—"

"Yes, church people are about the best people you'd ever want to meet," Doc began again.

I could see he was trying to avoid a sermon, but Jean asked, "Was that Mrs. Bennett, Scruggs?"

"Sure," he said. "Isn't she great? Anyway, Doc, I was a pretty miserable kid, and I didn't get the big idea about it—the Bible and all that. I thought—"

"Really, Scruggs, I'm just not interested!" Doc said.

Scruggs looked blank for a second, and then he just said, "Oh."

Doc was kind of embarrassed for being that abrupt. The rest of the ride passed in awkward silence. I guess he felt pretty bad for talking to Scruggs that way, because when we pulled up to the farmhouse at 4:30 P.M., he gave us the hour before dinner to row on the lake. In no time at all Scruggs and Jack dug the orange life jackets out of the farmhouse cellar.

We carried the wooden oars down to the pier behind the farmhouse. On the bank lay Doc's silver aluminum rowboat. We pushed it into the water, and Scruggs set the oars into the oarlocks.

He rowed. Jean and I sat in the stern, with Jack in the bow to navigate.

"You know," Scruggs said as he pulled back on the oars, "I hope I didn't get Doc mad because I tried to witness to him."

"I don't think he's mad," I said. "But it's like talking about God makes him feel really embarrassed. I think a lot of people are that way."

"I guess you're right," Scruggs said.

He pulled us out into the middle of the lake.

"This is great!" Jack said. "Sure beats getting up at the crack of dawn!"

Tracking Down Clues

Jean huddled down into her jacket. "I'm freezing."

"It does feel colder on the water," I said.

Scruggs grinned and pulled back on the oars. "Not to me! Keep your eyes along the lake shore, Penny and Jean. Jack, tell me if we're getting into water that's too shallow!"

"Okay. You can get closer to shore," Jack told him. We edged in closer. The wind wasn't sharp, but it felt cold, I suppose from the wetness. I wished for my gloves and scarf. Jean huddled down and looked pretty miserable, but she didn't say anything more about it.

"Anything?" Scruggs asked.

"We need field glasses," I told him. I could see houses, along the edge of Winneca Lake, and we came right up to some piers to get a good look at driveways and cars. But there was no sign of a yellow VW.

"It's been a long time," Scruggs grunted as he rowed. "Better turn back."

The light was fading under the trees along the shore. Scruggs turned us in a narrow part of the lake, and we came back along the opposite shore.

"Hey!" Jack exclaimed.

"What?" I asked.

"A telescope!"

Scruggs backed water to stop us but didn't look impressed. "So?"

"Row back a bit. Look," Jack said as Scruggs did so. "That house—there's a telescope popping out of the back window on the second floor!"

"No crime to use a telescope at night," Scruggs observed.

"It's pointed at the island," Jack said. "Not at the sky."

We were all silent. The boat started to drift, and Scruggs used an oar to keep it in place.

"It just moved," Scruggs said. "Someone's behind the curtain, using it."

"I still can't see it," Jean told him, and squinted at the two-story, brown-stained house.

"It's on us!" Scruggs cried.

"Come on," Jack said. "They've seen us."

Scruggs pulled on the oars, but even as we plowed through the water, I saw the eye of the telescope follow us.

"This is creepy," Jean observed.

"They're watching us," I warned.

"Can't go any faster," Scruggs told me, but in a second or two we were at least a better distance away, though—I knew—in plain sight of a telescope.

"Anybody up there would have a clear view of the pier on the island," Jack said. "What else?"

"Nothing but the woods around Pasture 4," I told him.

"Maybe it's a kid who owns the telescope," Jean guessed. "And he likes llamas."

"I don't know," Scruggs said. "Fake camp supervisors, hushed-up records of a flood, and a lot of accidents add up to a big mystery to me."

Chapter Sixteen
The Sheriff Again

We were so chilled by the time we got to our pier that the thought of hot food pushed away thoughts of a mystery.

We took off the life jackets and trooped up to the house. Jean's glasses fogged up as soon as we got inside.

"Here come the sailors, home from the sea!" Doc called out as we came in. "Look who's here, kids."

Sheriff Duncan grinned at us. "Looks like you've been out where it's cold," he said.

"Hot chili and sourdough bread in a minute," Mrs. Duncan promised. "Did you detectives find anything out on the lake?"

Jack looked chagrined. "How come people always know when we're looking for clues?" he asked me in a whisper. "Are we that transparent?"

"As glass," I told him.

"This never happens to Amy Belle," he mumbled. "She gets right in the middle of mysteries, and grown-ups hardly notice what she's up to. Like in *The Moon Surface Oil Rig Caper*—there she was, bouncing around in her space suit—"

105

I think he would have gone on, but just then Scruggs said to Sheriff Duncan, "Have you come to tell us more surprises about this island? I'm starting to think that anything might have happened here."

"Well, you know, it's funny you should mention that," Sheriff said. "I wasn't going to say anything, but I did find out some more puzzling things about the place. Of course, it was years ago—"

"What?" all four of us asked at once.

"Before you go into all that, have dinner!" Mrs. Ericson exclaimed.

So we sat around the table, said grace, and the sheriff talked to us. "I was pretty fresh outta high school, then. I wasn't sheriff, but I was on Highway Patrol. When the island flooded, I did rescue work, not investigation." He stopped long enough to fill up his bowl with chili and take a piece of sourdough bread. "It was days later when I found out that the camp wasn't licensed and that the husband and wife who'd run it had vanished. But do you know what? The FBI got in on the case, too. Naturally I didn't much care at first. But there was a whole month there when the island was closed to everybody."

"Would that be unusual?" Scruggs asked. "I mean, it was a big catastrophe."

"A month is a long time," Sheriff told him. "You see, even *we* couldn't come on the island without a pass. Nobody could. And the investigators carted stuff away in their trucks. But we never heard the story."

"So there *was* a mystery!" Scruggs said.

"Why didn't you tell us this before?" Doc asked.

"Well, last time, when I told you about the flood, you got so upset that I didn't go on," Sheriff told him.

The Sheriff Again

"I didn't want to add to your troubles." He put a spoonful of chili into his mouth, chewed it, swallowed, and said, "See, most folks who knew the FBI had come figured there'd been a murder or something—which wasn't true—but I didn't want you thinking that either. Didn't see any point in spooking you."

"We're adapting," Doc said. "Nothing's turned out like we imagined it would, but times haven't been all bad. I think we can run the risk of living with the history of this place."

Sheriff grinned. "And living with the jinx?"

"That, too." Doc glanced at his watch. "Penny and Jean, first shift at the barnyard," he said. "It's late, so you'd better get started."

"Right, Doc," I said, and we pushed back from the table.

Jean and I put on extra sweaters under our jackets and went down to the barn.

"What about flashlight tag?" she asked me as we went down the slope to the barnyard.

"I guess Jack and Scruggs'll come down once the dishes are done," I told her. "One of us can play and one can watch."

"We could toss a coin," she suggested.

I shrugged. "Nah, I'll let you play. Next time you watch while I play."

"Thanks."

We got into the barnyard, closed off the other gates, and settled down on the back of the hay wagon.

"You know what?" Jean said.

"What?"

"The only time you ever hear lots and lots of stuff about FBI cases is after they catch their crooks."

107

"Hmm?"

"I mean, you never hear newspaper reports that say, 'The FBI is now hot on the trail of a spy who's been avoiding them for five years.' You only hear of things that are finished."

"So?" I asked her.

"It's just that nobody in town knows why the federal investigators got involved in the island catastrophe. That might mean that the FBI is still working on the case. Only it's been so long that nobody cares anymore."

"I hadn't thought of that," I said.

"It may not be an old mystery at all," Jean said. "It might still be going on."

I shivered. "That gives me the creeps."

"Here come Jack and Scruggs," she said.

Jack and Scruggs and Jean played flashlight tag for about an hour. I'd started to wish I hadn't been so kind to Jean as to allow her to go off and play while I sat alone in the barnyard. But when they came back, she promised me she'd watch next time.

Jack and Scruggs went up to the bunkhouse to hit the hay before their watches started.

In the dark, thoughts of telescopes watching us were even creepier. I was glad Jean was there, but she didn't say much as the night got lonelier. At last Jack came down to relieve us, and on the way back to our room, Jean said, "It sure is easier to have a mystery when the sun is up."

Chapter Seventeen
Beans Has a Lesson

The next day dawned clear and cool. We concentrated on clearing out parts of Pasture 4. First we had to shoo some of the llamas out of our ash piles.

Like I've said, part of Pasture 4 is wooded, and there were rocks and old bits of mortar and hunks of wood all among the trees. We had to carry them to clear places so Doc could easily collect the rubble in the front-end loader and so that we could burn the wood without catching any trees on fire. We were all glad when the dinner gong rang for lunch.

After lunch, we went down to get the sulky.

"I've got an idea," Jack said. "But I'm not sure you're going to like it."

"What is it?" Scruggs asked.

"Hitch Beans to the sulky and then tie him so he can't go forward. Then keep the feed in front of him."

"We could try," Scruggs said, and I agreed.

Jack glanced at Jean. "What do you think?"

She was a little surprised at the question, but then she said, "Sure. It might work."

"Okay, then, let's get started." And Jack went off to get the sulky. I ran after him to help. "You're a great brother," I told him as I grabbed one of the gee poles.

"Aw, you're just saying that 'cause it's true," he said with a grin, but then he admitted, "I guess I know when I'm licked. If Jean's supposed to be a member of the team, she's supposed to be a member of the team. And she was the one who put her finger on the problem: Beans doesn't respect our commands because he thinks we can't make him obey."

There was some confusion about how to tie Beans. In the end we tied the sulky to the fence, running the ropes under the axle and fastening them to the gee poles. Jean took the driver's seat, and Scruggs and I took his head. Jack came out of the barn with the feed bucket.

"Whoa," Jean said as Beans started up. Scruggs and I held him, and he tried to shake us off as he leaped forward. But halfway into his first leap the tied sulky pulled him back.

"Whoa!" Jean said sternly. Jack disappeared back into the barn.

"Think he learned it?" Scruggs asked.

We backed him up to give the rope some slack. After a minute or two Jack came out again, and Beans stepped forward.

"Whoa!" Jean exclaimed, and pulled on the reins. He still didn't want us to hold him, but he was too smart to leap forward. Instead, he tried to slowly pull the sulky.

"Whoa," Jean insisted, and since the sulky didn't go anywhere, Beans stopped after a few seconds.

We backed him up again. It's important not to wear a llama down with training; so we only did it a few

Beans Has a Lesson

more times before we turned him loose and rewarded him with grain.

We gave him an hour's rest while we polished the sulky and swept out the barns.

"I bet he'll have it by next week," Jack said. "He'll make a great pacer."

He was right. In fact, that same afternoon Scruggs and I quit holding him. We lengthened the tie ropes that held the sulky to the fence. That way he could walk farther before Jean whoa'd him. By the end of the second session, he would stop on command.

"Now all we need to do is get him curried and groomed and we can show him off to Doc and Mrs.," Jack said as we unhitched him.

Scruggs glanced at his watch. "Well, it's three-thirty now. We won't have time. Maybe next week."

"That way we could give him a refresher on all his commands," Jean added. "To make sure it goes well."

"And next week we have to figure out a way to get closer to that house," Jack added. "To see if we can spot the yellow VW."

"We may have to dock at a distance and walk up through the trees," Scruggs said. "Well, we can decide later. Right now we better get up to the bunkhouse and get ready to go."

Of course it was hard during the week to think about school and homework with the llamas and telescopes and the VW on our minds. Jack walked around the house quoting from my Amy Belle books.

"You've read that whole series," I told him at last. "Even while you were making fun of it, you read every single book as fast as I got them."

He bowed. "I confess, Penny, I did. There's something in those books that keeps you reading. Don't ask me what. But, alas, Amy Belle was indeed my first love."

"Oh, cut it out," I said.

Friday afternoon came at last. We kept our overnight bags in the school office so that Doc could pick us up at school.

"What's new?" Jack asked as we climbed in.

"Trespassers last Sunday," Doc told him. "The very day after you left."

"In the pasture?" Jack asked.

"No, down in the trees along the shore. Older man and his wife. They said they were closing up their summer cabin and were out on one last rowboat trip. Said they'd wanted to get a look at the llamas."

"That sounds reasonable," Scruggs said.

"It was," Doc agreed. "But I told them we'd been having troubles lately, and I said I'd have to ask them to get off the premises. Told them we'd be open for tours next time they came up to the lake."

"Did they get mad?" Jack asked.

"Oh no, they were very apologetic. I felt like I'd been an ogre, but it can't be helped. If I could have workers all over the island, I wouldn't worry about curious people coming by. But when it's just me and my wife, we have to be careful."

"Will it be okay for us to take the boat out again today?" Scruggs asked.

Doc gave us a quick glance. "You kids found anything out on the lake?"

We all looked at each other. "We think so—maybe," I said. I told him about the telescope.

Beans Has a Lesson

He hid a grin. "You've been reading too many of those books you're always talking about—Annie what's-her-name."

"Amy Belle," I said.

"Well, don't make a nuisance of yourselves," he told us. "I don't think that telescope adds up to anything other than a stargazer. What good could anybody get from watching the island at that end?"

"That's true," Scruggs said, agreeing reluctantly. "Even the llamas don't bother much with Pasture 4. If someone wanted to hijack the herd or sneak by the house, they'd have to watch the other end of the island."

"All the same," Jack said, "as long as we're around, we may as well row past—"

"Sure, sure," Doc told him. "But I want a promise: no snooping around that house. If you should spot the yellow VW, get back to me or straight to the sheriff. Okay? *No* snooping on land."

We all glanced at each other.

"Come on, now," Doc said. "I want to hear four 'Yes, sirs' loud and clear."

"Yes, sir," Jean agreed.

"Yes, sir," Jack said.

"Yes, sir," I said.

Scruggs sighed a little. "Just when I got to like mysteries and stuff," he said. But he nodded. "Yes, sir, no snooping on land."

"Cheer up," Doc said. "If you guys get Beans to pull the cart this week, I'll give you each a bonus. And we'll get sundaes on the way home. Okay?"

"Yes, sir!" we all exclaimed.

113

Chapter Eighteen
An Adventure Despite Precautions

We hustled right out to the boat as soon as we got our gear stowed and had donned the life jackets. Jack had brought binoculars with him this time.

"Even if we can't go on land," he said, "we can try to get a glimpse of who's using the telescope."

"Or be glimpsed in our turn," Scruggs added as we clambered into the boat. We pushed off, and he brought us away from the island pier in strong, steady strokes. Since Jack had to watch to navigate, I took the field glasses.

I swept them up the far shore, and at first I couldn't even spot the house where the telescope belonged. But at last I did sight it.

"No telescope today," I said.

"Let's go in closer," Jack urged.

Scruggs glanced over at him. "Nothing doing. We promised Doc. We've got to try to be a good testimony to him."

"I didn't say to go on land," Jack told him. "Just row closer."

"Well, there's no yellow VW there," I said, watching through the glasses. "So we may as well keep our distance."

"Let me see," Jean said, and I handed the glasses to her. "Hey! There it is! Poked through the curtains!" We all jumped to grab the binoculars to look, and the boat nearly capsized.

"Easy!" Scruggs exclaimed.

Jack took the glasses. "Rats! All that commotion got their attention. The telescope's swinging around on us."

"Let's go, then," Scruggs said. He dipped the oars back into the water.

"They know now that we're keeping a watch on them," I observed as Scruggs rowed us back to the island.

"It couldn't be helped," Scruggs said with a grunt as he pulled on the oars. "And they started it by watching us."

"Oh, let's go!" Jean exclaimed. "It gives me chills to know someone's watching us."

"We're going as fast as we can, Jean," I said, but Scruggs smiled at her.

"No sweat," he said and pulled harder on the oars until beads of perspiration showed on the edge of his hairline. "Nothing to be scared of," he said between strokes. "They can't do anything to us in broad daylight."

But for her sake he hurried back to the pier and the safety of our island. We all went up to the house together and doffed the life jackets.

"You're back soon," Mrs. Ericson said as we came tramping into the kitchen.

An Adventure Despite Precautions

Doc was setting the table. "Looks like the detectives got thwarted," he said. "What happened? Somebody scold you?"

I told him what happened while we gave them a hand with dinner.

"Now, don't you four go getting yourselves spooked," he warned us. "You've got to be fit for the night watch, and I don't want you jumping at shadows."

Well, he was right to warn us, because even before we got down to the barn for our watch, Jean was jumpy and nervous. A wind had come up, and leaves rustled, and the hay whispered, and the llamas themselves couldn't settle down. They kept testing the wind.

At last Jack and Scruggs came down with the flashlight. Jean looked alarmed, as though she'd forgotten her promise to let me go out and play tag that night.

"Well," I said—but I said it grudgingly—"I don't have to go, if you're scared." I said it just the right way so that it would seem an insult if she really were scared.

"No, I'm all right," she said, rather faintly. "You can go out and play. I'll be okay."

I guess I did feel bad for Jean, but I really did want to play; so I ran off with Jack and Scruggs.

Jack was it, and he counted to ten while Scruggs and I dashed off. I got pretty far out in Pasture 1—almost to the fence that bordered Pasture 2, in fact—before he stopped counting. Quick as a wink I jumped the fence and flopped onto the ground, pressed as close to the hog-wire as I could get. I was hoping he'd swing the flashlight beam high and miss where I was at the foot of the fence.

It almost worked. I lay absolutely still and watched the beam flick around the field. Jack was singing, "Oh, where, oh, where has my Penny gone? Oh, where, oh, where can she be?" Then he yelled, "Come on, Scruggs! I see you there, pretending to be a tree stump! Oh! It's a tree stump that was pretending to be Scruggs."

But at last the beam came zigzagging around me, and as Jack got close, he finally spotted me and swung the beam on me.

"Ha!" he cried. "Good thing I read *Amy Belle and the Treasure in the Fence-Post Factory!* I might never have thought to look along the fence, otherwise."

He came through the wide gate.

"You better shut it," I said. Since things had calmed down again, we had started letting the llamas stay in Pasture 1 at night, but I didn't think it was wise to let them get out to Pasture 2.

"Oh, the llamas are in the barnyard. They don't come out this far at night," he said with a shrug.

I walked with him through Pasture 2, but there was no sign of Scruggs.

"That rat, he's gone into the woods in Pasture 4," Jack said. "I bet he's gone up a tree. We'll never catch him."

We went through to Pasture 4, and it was so lonely and desolate and creepy out there that Jack left that gate open, and I didn't protest. Somehow I didn't want a closed gate between me and the safety of the barnyard. And Jack muttered, "That Scruggs has got guts. I sure wouldn't hide way out here."

Just then a wild scream split the air. I grabbed Jack's arm.

An Adventure Despite Precautions

"Jack!" I yelled, but just then the scream broke into laughter.

"Up here, you clowns!"

I could tell that Jack had shivered, but he gave me a stern glance and pulled away. He flicked the light up the nearest tree, and there was Scruggs, laughing at us. He swung down from the tree.

"Scruggs," I said. "I bet poor Jean heard that all the way at the barn."

He still thought it was funny, but when I said that, he nodded. "Let's go tell her it's okay, then."

"Suits me," I said. "This grass is damp out here. There's a path to the gate up this way." I only took about five steps, and the last words I heard were Jack's: "Hey, Penny, look out!"

And then my foot walked on air. I fell forward, yelled, heard a terrific thump and at the same moment felt my head and shoulder blades hit the ground so hard it knocked the wind out of me right before it knocked me out.

Chapter Nineteen
We Stumble into Danger

The next thing I knew, aside from a headache and the feeling that all my bones had been jarred loose, was that Jack was by me in a dark place.

"Are you okay?" he was whispering. "Are you okay?"

I tried to move and it hurt, but not dreadfully. I'd landed all in a tumble.

"I think so."

He put his arms around me and got me sitting up. I had one bad moment of dizziness, but then I got better. The clear, cold air helped me get my head together.

"Where are we?" I asked.

"You fell into one of the old foundations," Jack said.

"Where's Scruggs?"

"Right here," Scruggs's voice said in the darkness. "Trying to find the easiest way for you to climb out. Can you stand?"

"I don't know."

Jack helped me up. "I guess I'm okay," I said. "But my head's ringing."

"There's a pile of rubble here," Scruggs said. "Shine a light, Jack."

Jack did, and Scruggs pulled away rotting beams, an old cinder block, and some dirt away from a pile of junk in a corner.

"Flood waters pushed all this together," he said. "Packed in pretty tight—I don't know if I can—hey!"

"What?" Jack asked.

"Crates," Scruggs said. "And a barrel."

"So?"

"They're half-rotted, but there's something inside them. Come here."

We all stepped closer.

Scruggs reached in with a nervous hand and got his fingers into one of the gaping cracks of a crate.

"Plastic," he said. "It's lined with plastic."

"Let's get it hoisted out of here," Jack said. He scrambled up the rubble and out of the hole. "Can you lift it?" he asked Scruggs.

Scruggs managed to lift the two rotting crates to Jack, and I helped him get a small barrel up. Then Scruggs helped me get out, and he followed.

I didn't feel that great, but I was eaten up with curiosity. We tilted the barrel so that it rested against the crates, and Scruggs got his fingers into a gaping crack in the lid. He pulled, and instead of getting the lid up, he merely tore away a wide strip of rotting wood.

"Plastic sheeting," I said. "Who's got a knife?"

Scruggs pulled out his jackknife and ripped open the thick sheeting. He thrust his hand inside and pulled out a handful of twenty-dollar bills.

"Money!" Jack cried. "We're rich!"

Scruggs looked amazed, too. "Crates and a barrel of money! How—" And then he stopped. "Wait a minute!

It's gotta be a fake," he said. "Or stolen. That would explain a lot—"

A voice interrupted him. "None of you move." And the beam of a powerful light shone on us. We all froze.

"Who is it?" Scruggs said at last.

"Go on, shoot," a man's voice said.

A second man's voice answered, "Are you *crazy?* That'd be murder."

And a woman's voice added, "Not here. They'd hear it at the house."

Jack slipped his hand over mine.

"This is it," Scruggs whispered. But as nothing happened, he called, "Who's there?"

"Shut up!" the woman's voice said. But the flashlight beam lowered a bit, and we saw three figures approaching. As they neared the glow from Jack's light, we could see that it was a gray-haired man, a gray-haired woman, and the young man we had been looking for. He didn't have his sunglasses on, and he was wearing dark clothing. But he looked scared.

"Who are you?" Jack asked.

"Take them to the rowboat," the older man said.

"Now look—" the younger one began.

"Do it!" the first one exclaimed.

"You aren't taking us anywhere," Scruggs said. But at his words the two older ones pulled out guns.

"It'd be pretty stupid to argue with this," the older man said. He reached forward and grabbed Scruggs by the shoulder. "Come on!"

The woman got me by the arm and pulled me after Scruggs, and the young man brought up the rear with Jack.

"We'll take them back to the house—" the old man said as he pulled Scruggs. "Would you quit dragging?" he hissed to the dark-haired man.

"No, go to the marshes," the woman said.

"I can't do this," their partner gasped. "You never said we'd have to do this. You said it was easy money. I can't use a gun on people. It was bad enough when you made me break into the house and—"

"You stole the key to the gun cabinet!" Jack exclaimed. "We might have known—" The old man pulled up his gun and leveled it at Jack. "Shut up." Then he pointed it at his own partner. The young man abruptly shut his mouth, too.

"What's it going to take to stop your whining? I've been waiting years to get this money, and nobody's gonna stop me," the old man said. "We're all in this all the way. You get it?"

"But he's right," Scruggs said to the old man. "We don't even know who you are. What—"

"Shut up!" the old man said, but just then a glow shone on us. We all looked back. A scent of kerosene hung in the air. Jean, illuminated by the disposable lighter she had in her hand, stood on top of the crates. The crates were dripping with kerosene. There'd been a can nearby, covered with bits of wood to protect it from rain.

"Run, Jean!" Scruggs said. The old man backhanded him and then leveled his gun at Jean.

"Get down from there!" he exclaimed.

Jean had the flame of the lighter turned all the way up.

"Shoot," she said.

We Stumble into Danger

Well, of course he couldn't do that, because if he did, she would drop the lighter and all that money would catch on fire.

"Get her down from there!" the older man hissed.

Their light was still trained on the path ahead. Jack's light was pointed down. Jean was illuminated only by her lighter.

Suddenly, as the woman ran forward, Jean's light winked out, and for a second none of us could see Jean because our eyes hadn't readjusted. Quick as a flash the crates and barrel roared up in a sheet of flame.

The woman jumped back, forgetting her gun.

"No! The money!" the old man screamed. Scruggs hit him, and Jack tackled him, too. He swung his flashlight across the man's hand, and the gun dropped.

Scruggs kicked it into the trees. "Let's get out of here!" he cried.

We three raced into the darkness, hopped the fence, and got into the trees.

"Jean," Scruggs whispered. "Where is she?"

"We've got to get back to her," Jack whispered.

I heard something. "Wait," I said. "Shhh."

We listened and heard a quiet rustling as someone made his way through the dark trees.

"Jean!" I whispered, and heard her answer.

"Where are you?" she whispered back. But in another second her dark form came down the path. We all hugged her.

"How did you do it?" Scruggs asked.

"I saw you find the money," she said. "But they were between us. I worked my way around to the kerosene can and dragged it up while they argued about what to do with you."

"Come on," Scruggs said. "We're not safe. Get down to the shore."

"They're trying to save the money," Jean said.

"Once the shock wears off, they'll be looking for an escape," Jack said.

We got to the shore and saw the boat they'd come up on. We pushed it into the water and were clambering aboard, when Scruggs said, "Here they come!" And their searchlight cut across the water.

"Dive!" Scruggs yelled. He grabbed Jean and went over the side. Jack and I followed, capsizing the boat. Bullets cut into the water, but they missed us by yards.

My heavy clothes and the frigid water dragged me down. But I felt a hand grab and pull me along until my feet touched bottom. My head broke water, and I tried not to gasp with the cold.

Silently Jack pulled me along in water that was shoulder high. The intruders, on the shore, had their light on the capsized boat, and their guns were ready.

We rounded a bend in the shore of the island.

"In," Jack gasped. We'd been in the water for about a minute and a half. I couldn't move my hands or feel Jack's hand on my arm. The killing water had pierced the insulation of my clothes.

We staggered in to shore.

"They'll get us," I whispered. "I'm so cold."

But from up on the island we could hear a snapping and rustling as though people were rushing to the fire. Behind us, we heard a splash as one of the intruders leaped into the water—probably to get the boat.

Scruggs had gotten to shore with Jean, but the frigid waters had sapped his strength.

"Someone's up there," Jack whispered.

"Llamas—the fire," Jean said.

"We've got to get to the house," Scruggs said. "Don't slap yourselves or jump around. Just move to the house!"

You might have to live in Wisconsin to understand how cold it can be on a night in October, and how deadly it can be to fall into cold lake water.

It was about 35 degrees on the shore, but the water—which had frozen and thawed during the week—had robbed us of body heat. That can happen in about a minute, and that's why you sometimes will see news accounts of swimmers who drown in shallow water. The water is too cold, and it numbs them.

We got our arms around each others' shoulders and walked to the house in a solid line. My mind seemed to switch off, but I do have a memory of a door opening and light spilling over me and hearing Mrs. Ericson's voice.

Chapter Twenty
Answers

I felt like a mummy when I opened my eyes, and then I realized that I was lying in a sleeping bag. I was warm and dry. At the moment that was enough; so I closed my eyes again.

But then I remembered Jean and Jack and Scruggs. I opened my eyes and struggled to get up.

"It's all right, Penny. We're here."

"Mom!" I exclaimed. "What—what day is it?"

"It's tomorrow," she said and kissed me.

"Where's Jean?" I asked.

Mom smiled at me. "Right beside you."

I turned and looked, and sure enough, there she was—snuggled in a sleeping bag on the bed with blankets over her. Her cheeks were rosy with warmth.

"What about Jack and Scruggs?" I asked.

"They're in the guest room," she said. She smoothed back my hair.

"Those people chased us. Jean saved us. We found money, Mom—"

"Sheriff Duncan's been out there," Mom said. "He thinks he's got it put together."

"The old couple—they were the ones who ran the camp," I said. "They were crooks all along."

"Yes," Mom told me. "And when the flood destroyed their operation and blew their cover, they escaped. But they left behind half a million dollars in stolen bills."

"And couldn't find it," I added. "The flood waters moved it, swept it somewhere."

She nodded. "All of the containers were banded together in twos. The FBI never found any. Once the Feldersons—that's the name of the old couple—found out that nobody else had found the money, they had to wait for the island to be 'safe' to visit. It took years of waiting, but as long as nobody moved onto the island, they didn't mind."

"And then they had to find the money without being caught," I added.

"Right. So they hired a younger man who wouldn't be recognized. It was his job to get onto the island in a legitimate way," she told me. "That was why he thought up an excuse to come out and survey the land. When that didn't work, he engineered a few 'accidents' to get everybody to concentrate on watching the herd while he and the other two searched the far pastures at night."

"But we found it without even looking," I said.

Mom smiled. "You only found part of it—less than half. And you weren't worried about being caught or about not letting your lights show. They had to be much more wary, and they were concentrating more on the woods than the fringe where you were. And even you wouldn't have found it unless Scruggs had started pulling apart that rubble."

"Doc caught them earlier by day," I said. "I'm sure it was the same couple."

Answers

Mom nodded. "You see, they saw you watching their house. They were in a hurry."

"Did they steal the money?"

She shook her head. "No. They laundered it. It was a regular business for them. For a large fee, they traded 'clean' money for all kinds of stolen money and for money won in illegal gambling games. Then they ran the 'dirty' money through the people who came to the camp. That way the money was dispersed all over the state and couldn't be traced back to the people who had gotten it."

"But—"

She leaned closer. "You need to rest," she said. "No more questions right now."

I fell asleep right away, and when I next woke up, Jean was half-awake.

"Hi," she said sleepily.

I felt a lot better and struggled out of the sleeping bag enough to sit up.

"How did you do that?" I asked her. "How did you think so fast? And to stand right there—"

She woke up more and sat up. "I prayed, for one thing," she said. "And I had the lighter in my pocket because I wanted to be in charge of the fires today out in the field." She sighed and then yawned. "And I knew they wouldn't shoot me if I was on top of the money with the lighter in my hand." She glanced at me. "I read a story once about a guy who offered himself in exchange for a hostage, but he strapped dynamite all over himself under his jacket so that the guys holding him captive didn't dare shoot him. That way he made them let their other hostage go. It was the same idea."

"And to think," I said, "you used to be a chicken."

"I still am," she told me. "I was really scared. But I acted cool like heroes in books always act. Until that lady ran at me. I got so scared I let the lighter button go and it went out. Then I jumped down, got it lit again, and tossed it on the pile. Then I ran." She looked around the room. "Where are we?"

"Doc and Mrs. Ericson's room," I told her.

"Are Scruggs and Jack okay?"

"Yeah, in the guest room."

"I think Scruggs saved my life," she said.

"I think the llamas saved all of us," I added. "The gates were open, and they came to the fire like bees to clover."

"How'd that save us?"

"Well, those crooks didn't look for us much, not once we swam away from the boat. I think they heard the llamas coming and thought they were people."

She nodded. "So all they wanted was to get away. Did they?"

"I don't know." And then I told her everything that Mom had told me—all about the money laundering operation.

"Ten years!" she exclaimed. "They waited that long?"

"Yeah, but you know what?" I asked. "I bet they were waiting to outwit both sides."

"Huh?"

"Well, people who launder money are usually working for organized crime—like the Mafia and groups like that," I told her.

"Yeah?"

"I think the Feldersons were trying to cheat both the FBI and organized crime," I told her. "When the flood came, and the money was swept away, they didn't

Answers

have to bother making an exchange of clean for dirty money. The flood let them off the hook. The operation was over, and the people they were working for figured the money was gone. So the Feldersons knew that whatever they could find, they could keep for themselves. But they had to be careful to make sure that the crooks they'd once worked for never suspected them. That's one reason it took so long," I guessed.

"I get it now." She groaned and kicked her way out of the sleeping bag, then swung out of the big, king-sized bed.

"Good night, whose pajamas are these?" she asked, looking down at the flannel pajamas that she had on. The sleeves came down to her knees, and the legs were so long that they trailed out behind her.

"Look like Doc's," I said. "I guess we got bundled into whatever was handy."

"Let's get dressed," she said. "Mom and Dad are here—I think I heard you talking with her a while ago. I want to go down and get something to eat."

Our clothes had been brought up. We changed and met Mom on our way out. She had a tray in her hands. "What's this?" she asked. "You should be in bed."

"We feel fine," I told her. "And we want to see Jack and Scruggs."

"Well, force yourselves to stay and eat this soup," she said, "and then we'll see."

Chapter Twenty-one
Really a Team

Jack and Scruggs were fine. Late in the afternoon, once Mom had called a doctor to make sure we would really be okay, we all came down to the living room. Sheriff Duncan came over, too, and he shook hands with each of us before he went out to check on a few things out on the grounds.

"Did you catch them?" Jean asked as he made for the door.

"Sure did," he said. "Doc described the older couple—he figured they were the ones he'd caught trespassing—and they were nabbed by the Highway Patrol, going into Minnesota." He shook his head. "You kids sure beat all the odds in getting out alive from that scrape."

"Prayer helps," Dad said and shot a glance at Doc.

"These kids are set on making a believer out of me," Doc said with a laugh, "and you, too!" But then he did look sober. "Well, to tell you the truth, when I saw them last night ready to drop from hypothermia, I guess I did pray. And," he added, "when I heard how they cheated the odds so much, I guess it did make me stop and think."

"You mean about God?" Scruggs asked. "Or do you think we got out of all that because we were just lucky?"

"There you go again," Doc said, and he grinned. "Trying to convert me."

Scruggs looked a little flustered. Jean piped up, "Do you think it was just luck that saved us?" she asked.

"Now look, kids, I'm not saying either way," he said. "But you're all going to have to grow up a little more before you try to save the world. Some people just don't talk about religion."

Dad shook his head. "I guess they've been through enough this weekend to have a say in what or who saved them," he said.

"Well, that's fine. Everybody's got an opinion," Doc said. "But I'm not a religious man; so they don't have to waste their breath. Excuse me while I see how dinner is coming." And he walked out.

"Boy," I said. "You try and try to be good and witness to someone and let him know what you believe, and then you almost get killed, and he still couldn't care less!"

"Sometimes it takes a whole lifetime," Dad said. "And sometimes the Lord might use something completely different. Remember the Apostle Paul?" he asked. "Paul had a hand in the deaths of plenty of martyrs, and their testimony didn't affect him. God intervened directly in his life."

"The important thing," Mom added, "is not to look at what you've done or what you've gone through, but to try to understand what the Lord is doing."

"And meanwhile," Dad said, "it really is a miracle that you came out of all that alive."

I turned to Jean. "Say, why *did* you come out to Pasture 4? It wasn't like you to leave your post."

"Well, really," she said, "I was nervous out there all by myself. And then I heard this terrible scream— it sounded like Scruggs. So I ran out to see if everything was okay."

"Scream?" Scruggs asked.

"When you played that joke on Jack and me," I said.

"I guess that tipped those three crooks off, too," Scruggs added. "But you'd think they'd have preferred to leave us alone. We'd have left in a minute."

"I think they did mean to leave us alone," I told him. "Until we started yelling about the money."

Jack slapped himself on the forehead. "That's right! What dopes we were! We brought them down on us. They knew they had to move then or never."

"Yeah, and they had to make sure we couldn't identify them," Scruggs said as he put his arm around his mother. Mrs. Bennett had—of course—come up with my folks. He looked at her and smiled. "Doc can say what he wants—I'm glad someone was praying for us. We'd have all been dead long ago, otherwise."

Jack glanced at him, and Scruggs laughed. "From the sulky!" he exclaimed.

"You have taken a few spills," Dad agreed.

We heard Sheriff coming back in through the kitchen doorway, and he and Doc came into the living room together.

"Hey, is that deal still good?" Jack asked. "Do we get a bonus if we can ride him around today with no problems?"

"Sure," Doc said. "Do you feel up to it?"

"Yes!" we all exclaimed.

"Go to it, then."

We went down to the barn.

Scruggs still looked a little chagrined because Doc wouldn't listen to us, and I guess I did, too, because he said to me, "I can't understand him either. You'd think that after he went and admitted that maybe God protected us he'd listen."

"Well, we have from now until winter to try again," I said. I wanted to be optimistic. "And then in the spring he might have us come back up on weekends—or maybe next summer we can stay through the weeks and get him and Mrs. Ericson to come to church."

"I hope so," he said. "And really," he admitted, "it's only been about eight weeks. I guess we ought to be more patient."

"Not everybody you witness to gets saved," I said after a minute. "At least not right away. And I guess sometimes they don't even want to listen."

He nodded. We let ourselves into the barnyard, and he and Jack brought Beans in, and we got him hitched to the cart.

"Only takes two at a time," Jack said. "How about one boy and one girl?"

I looked at Jean. I really wanted to go in the cart, but it was Jean who had rescued us. And besides, if we were supposed to be a team, I knew I ought to let her do what she wanted on this, because that's the way it is on a team. "You go," I said. "You deserve it." And it was odd, because as soon as I said it, I was really glad Jean had come. Sure she could be a chicken, but she was a pretty smart kid.

"You too, Scruggs," Jack said. "It shouldn't be all Derwoods in the cart."

"No," Scruggs said. "I'll wait 'til next time. You go. It was your idea to tie the sulky, and that was what finally broke Beans."

"Really—" Jack said.

"Come on, get in," Scruggs told him. "We'll all have our fill of driving it. Just do a good job, okay? I want that bonus."

Jack glanced at me, and I nodded. "Okay," he said and climbed in. He held out his hand to Jean as she climbed in. And this time I don't think he minded that she was with him.

We opened the gate for them, and Jack clucked with his tongue. Beans pranced up the dirt road to the house.

Everyone came out on the porch to watch. Beans turned perfectly and came back up the road by the machine shed. The Ericsons clapped, and Doc came down to watch Beans bring the cart back down to the barn.

"Whoa!" Jack said, and Beans stopped and stood as still as a post while Jack and Jean clambered down.

"Great!" Doc said. "I guess you get your bonus. Put your gear up and come on back to the house."

We let Beans loose in Pasture 1 and brought all the tack back into the barn.

"Good job," Scruggs said.

We all walked up the dirt road to the house.

"This is even better than *Amy Belle and the Secret of the Holstein Cow*," Jack said. "She drove a horse in that book, but *we* drove llamas!"

"Yeah, and we make a good team," Scruggs added. He looked at Jean. "Right, Short Stuff?"

"Right!" she said.

I saw Jack look at them, and then he looked at me. He smiled. "Right!"

I smiled back. "Right!" I added.